Hallelujah
Chariot

by Evelyn Hathaway

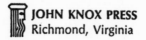
JOHN KNOX PRESS
Richmond, Virginia

To Mamma and Papa
Who maketh the clouds his chariot:
who walketh upon the wings of the wind.
Psalm 104:3

Standard Book Number: 8042-2080–8
Library of Congress Catalog Card Number: 72–79924
© M. E. Bratcher 1969
Printed in the United States of America

Contents

A story drawn from
the life of my father,
Dr. Andrew O. Hendricks.
"A man's work is the portrait of his soul."

1

The Long, Long Ford

"Well, hallelujah! Will ya just look at that! It's a regular chariot." Little Frankie Becker, who lived across the street, dashed over just as Pastor Hendricks, with a proud flourish and a toot of the big bulb horn, piloted the new Ford up the driveway. With that impromptu remark Frankie had christened the new car.

Instantly, the pastor's five children tumbled out of the back door of the house and down the steps, pushing and pulling at each other in their excitement. All mouths fell open as they reached the bottom of the stairs and had their first real view of the long, long Ford.

The new 1917 Model T, basically a Ford touring car, looked like a dachshund with a unique breeding all its own. It had been elongated in the center, allowing the addition of six jump seats. It was the longest vehicle any of the children had ever seen. Later, if some of the neighborhood children didn't get to ride in it as often as they wanted, they gave it disdainful looks and called it an "old weiner dog." Now the pastor's brood walked slowly around it, inspecting it thoroughly. They explored its shiny surface with their fingers while they talked and yelled all at once. It was a case of love at first sight.

In the midst of all the confusion, Fawn and Minnie, the housekeeper, came out on the porch. Minnie, whose thick Swedish accent added to the clamor, quickly ran down to join the children. But Fawn stopped suddenly at the edge of the steps. She put one hand against her breast as if to hold herself erect. "What," she said softly, "has Andrew brought home now?" She had expected a beautiful new Ford, resplendent with brass lamps and fittings, like any of those driven by members of the congregation. The pastor of one of the largest churches in Los Angeles certainly ought to set a conservative tone in his choice of an automobile. But there, confronting her, was a stretched-out metal monster with her husband standing by it protectively, a rather guilty smile on his face. He was trying to whistle nonchalantly as he dusted the headlights with his handkerchief. Fawn continued to stare, first at Andrew, then at the automobile, and then back at Andrew again.

His wife's silence was more than Andrew had bargained for. The whistling stopped. Waiting for her comment, he shot quick glances at her from under his dark eyebrows while pretending to be engrossed in his polishing. He knew all too well what type of car Fawn had expected. But he thought it the better part of valor to wait until she spoke before attempting an explanation of his strange purchase.

The children hadn't noticed Papa's uneasiness or Mamma's silence. They inspected their new car with raucous cheers.

"Boy, oh boy!" nine-year-old Bud yelled. "This is a regular trolley car."

"No," corrected Sistie with an elegant toss of her long blonde hair. "It's a limousine. At least we can call it that. It's as long as one anyway." Sistie was eleven and the oldest. She was already a little lady.

"No sirree, it's a Chariot," Lolly insisted loudly, hanging over one of the doors and swinging vigorously back and forth. She was a tomboyish seven. "It's our very own Chariot."

Duck and Pidge, four and two respectively, were happily exploring the roomy interior, while they mentally counted the extra friends it would hold. Duck said breathlessly, "She'll take a hundred kids I betcha."

Lolly, in a rare practical mood, counted the seats. "No, but we can take twenty-four if every passenger will hold somebody on his lap."

Fawn had decided she might as well find out the worst. "Andrew, did you really *buy* this thing?" she said, coming down the steps.

He nodded his head. "Fawn dear, it was a real bargain. That's because it's not a standard model. An amateur inventor made it with the idea of selling it to a private school. When he was finished, he thought it was too handsome to do service as a bus. He put it up for sale just this morning as a family-style limousine."

Fawn remained silent.

Andrew grinned his boyish grin. "I thought of all the people we've always wanted to take to church," he rattled on hastily, "and all the neighborhood children we could take to Sunday school. It seemed an answer to prayer, Fawn; I just couldn't pass it up."

Fawn didn't answer. Minnie, seeing the disappointment on her face and the worried look in Andrew's eyes, shooed the children into the house to get washed for supper.

Fawn waited on the steps while Andrew drove the Chariot into the garage. Half of it stuck out through the doors. He got out and stood stroking his chin thoughtfully. Fawn knew from experience the meaning of that look. Andrew was figuring out a way to add to the garage. For him this would be no problem. He had always been a genius at enlarging everything they owned, so that they might share it with the world. Her eyes dwelt on her husband with loving resignation. "If I could be just half that generous!" she sighed, shaking her head.

At the dinner table that evening Fawn was not herself. Ordinarily she presided over the long table with lively skill and tact, mingling the conversations of adults and children so that everybody had a chance to speak and no one was ever bored. But tonight she was quiet. She had loved their old Ford. She had hoped that it would be replaced by one just like it, certainly not the monstrosity that Andrew had brought home.

She glanced around the table. The children, sensing her mood, were quiet, too. Even Andrew had given up trying to pretend things were the same as usual. Fawn had been a pastor's wife much too long not to realize how very practical the car would be. She seemed to notice their long faces for the first time; hers lit up with a smile.

"Children," she said gaily, "whom shall we invite to be the first to ride in the new car?" With Fawn's changing mood, the uneasy silence was broken and everyone suddenly found plenty to talk about.

Even without the excitement of the new car, dinner would have been a rather hectic affair. The church had been having a series of special meetings and tonight Andrew was going to tell the story of his life for the first time from the pulpit. There was a great deal of their father's youth about which the children had heard only vague, tantalizing references. They knew that once he had had tuberculosis and typhoid fever. They had heard something about a miracle being involved in his healing, but the details of the story were not clear to them, and for good reason.

Andrew and Fawn had deliberately refrained from discussing his experience with them. They knew, all too well, the show-off tendencies of their brood and how such a story would grow with each telling as they related it to the neighbor children for blocks around. Andrew had prudently waited until he thought that they were old enough to understand the sanctity of what had happened to him. After much prayer and discussion, he and Fawn had decided that the children should attend tonight's meeting.

The minute dinner was over, Fawn rushed upstairs to change her own clothes and those of the two younger boys. Minnie good-naturedly left her dishes to supervise Lolly, Sistie, and Bud, as they washed and dressed in their Sunday best. After she had looked behind their ears, checked their pockets for clean handkerchiefs, and helped them on with their coats, they rushed out to join Andrew. He had changed into his swallow-tailed suit and was now waiting at the front curb in the new automobile. Impatiently he pulled up and down on the spark lever, making the engine roar. He hoped the noise might hurry Fawn, but it didn't.

Fawn knew they had plenty of time. She didn't come out of the front door until satisfied that her appearance was impeccable, with every hair in place. Utterly disregarding Andrew's undignified antics, she led Duck and Pidge in a leisurely approach to the snorting automobile. Andrew had to admit that Fawn looked extremely fetching in her trim, black broadcloth suit reaching nearly to the ground and he beamed at her happily as he opened the door. Fawn gave him an indulgent smile, as in her own unhurried, regal way she stepped for the first time into the Chariot.

When the car was finally humming along at thirty miles an hour, Andrew glanced over at Fawn. She was looking straight ahead; her right hand clutched her wide-brimmed moline hat so it wouldn't be whipped off her head by the wind. His hand stole over to her knee, where he tapped his fingers three times. This was their secret signal for "I love you." Fawn looked at him from the corner of her eye. She slipped her free arm from around Duck, who sat between them, walked her fingers across the back of the seat to his shoulder, and tapped Andrew three times.

Andrew sighed; now he could whistle again.

The ride to the church was a real thrill to the children because of the way people stared as the Chariot whizzed by. The children reveled in the attention they were receiving. But Andrew was too busy to notice as he threaded his way through the traffic of automobiles and horses and buggies that clogged the main street of Los Angeles.

Carriages, automobiles, and bicycles were lined up for blocks. Parishioners and visitors had come early to get a good seat in the "mother church" of the Nazarene faith. People were streaming up the steps and crowding in the huge front doors as Andrew nosed the long car into the stall marked "Pastor." The children giggled uncontrollably. A crowd gathered around to have a look at the pastor's big, new, unusual automobile.

They all piled out. Andrew reached to the floor of the car and took out a long strap which had fastened to it an iron collar with a big spike. Then he locked one end of the strap to the steering wheel, leaned down and drove the spike into the mortar between the bricks of the driveway, and clamped the collar around the front tire.

Fawn asked, "Andrew, what on earth is that thing for?"

Andrew stooped again and pointed. "That's called a boot. If anyone tries to drive the automobile away without removing it," he explained, "the thumping will attract attention. Then everyone will know the car is being stolen."

"Oh!" Fawn said in an amazed voice. "Do you really think anyone else would want this automobile?"

Andrew smiled, "Now Fawn, dear, you'll get used to it in time; wait and see."

The children were reluctant to leave their new car, but

Fawn hurried them into the church. The choir was already taking its place as they scurried up to the balcony. Fawn insisted they always sit in the same place so she could keep an eagle eye on them from her place just below the choir loft. The children liked the balcony. They all had a lively curiosity and the balcony afforded them a bird's-eye view of everything that went on.

The church was filled to capacity. The congregation had known of the story of his miracle, but was eager to hear it from his lips. Also, there were many in the audience who had come to hear Fawn sing.

When the hymn singing was finished, it was Andrew's custom to introduce from the platform any notable visitors. Tonight several professors were present, also some of Andrew's colleagues on the city council. They had come to hear the story of his life. They regarded him respectfully but with curiosity. To them he was a zealot with a sense of humor and a broad educational background. Touched by the Christian example which Andrew quietly but un-deviatingly lived from day to day, they were eager to know what had influenced him.

After the introductions, Fawn sang Andrew's favorite, "The Old Rugged Cross." Then Andrew stepped forward and began his story:

"Ever since I have been pastor of this church, I have often been asked to tell the story of my life. After much prayer and searching of my heart, I decided to do so tonight. I do this for two reasons: first, in hopes that the telling may encourage someone to answer the call to go into God's service. Second, that you may see that God can use anyone—even a hardheaded, ignorant Swedish farmboy like myself. I also hope," Papa said with a rueful smile, "that none of you has to go through the same ordeal as I, in order to be of use to God.

"I was born in Sweden and christened Andrew Olaf Hendrickson." Andrew cleared his throat and put his hands behind him. "My parents, Olaf and Kristina Hendrickson, brought me to this country. We were Swedish Huguenots. My father wanted to be more American, so he dropped the 'son' from our name. My brothers and sisters and I grew up on a farm in Minnesota. I worked hard and I played hard, too, when I got the chance—which wasn't often. I was not much different from dozens of Swedish farmboys growing up around me, except for one thing. One day when I was seventeen, God spoke to me. He asked me a question and I made him a promise.

"That day came as the climax of a tragic time for my family. My father had been killed in an accident on the farm. Then, a short while later my baby sister died of appendicitis. My mother was a strong woman, but her grief, coming on top of so many years of hard work had made her old beyond her span. They found out that I was ill with an advanced case of tuberculosis, complicated by typhoid fever. This discovery nearly prostrated her. Unable to care for me herself, she and my older brother Nels took me to a sanitarium in nearby Battle Lake.

"It was there that God changed my life. I shall never forget that hospital room. You see, I was about to die and I knew it. . . ."

2

The Boy

I was coughing and couldn't seem to stop. I was vaguely aware of someone holding me tightly but gently over a small basin. "It must be Dr. Jones," I thought. I opened my eyes for a moment, blearily noticing the bright, bubbly pink blood I had just coughed up swirling around in the basin.

"This is the worst hemorrhage he's had," said Nurse Swanson in a voice filled with concern. Dr. Jones laid me back on the mound of pillows. I was too tired to keep my eyes open and sank into a semi-stupor. The nurse walked across the room and stood by the door. In a moment the doctor joined her. They obviously thought I was unconscious and couldn't hear a word they were saying.

"He's going to die, isn't he?" the nurse whispered.

"Yes, he's going to die," Dr. Jones replied. "I don't see how he's lasted this long."

"Die!" I thought wonderingly at first and then fearfully. "I'm going to die!" In a panic I concentrated on trying to catch what the doctor and nurse were saying.

"How on earth did a young boy like this get tuberculosis, Doctor?"

"Well, I have his case history from his family physician. It apparently started after his father died."

The doctor's voice droned on in the distance, but all I could think about were the words, "Yes, he is going to die." Somewhere I had heard those exact words before. They had been spoken about my father and my father *had* died. My head spun around and around. I clutched the sheet, trying to quell my terror. I was remembering my father's death. A tree had fallen on him when he was clearing some land.

My father's body was laid out in the parlor. Mother and the neighbors took turns sitting up with the corpse. My brothers and sisters—Nels, Anna, Jo, Astrid, John— and I stayed away from the front room. We were afraid of the dead.

After the service Dr. Copes took Mother outside, and we children trailed along behind. He was a short, stocky man with blue eyes and a thatch of silvery hair.

"My dear Kristina," he said, shaking his head sadly. "Your husband was in the prime of life at forty-two. It looked to me as if he were trying to build a whole new world in one day. If he had taken life a little easier and hadn't been so obsessed with clearing this land and putting up all of these big buildings, he would be alive today. Something will happen to you too, if you continue to drive yourself trying to keep up this big farm. Without Olaf it is an impossibility, Kristina. Sell this place. It will bring enough money to tide you over until the boys are grown. These children are working much too hard. You owe it to them to leave here."

Kristina, my mother, was a tall woman with the commanding presence of a Viking. Her dark eyes and black hair she had inherited from her French Huguenot ancestors. With her chiseled features and straight lips, her hair pulled back and braided in a chignon at the nape of her neck, she looked every inch a Swedish Huguenot as her glance swept Father's fields and buildings. They rested for a moment on the tree under which her husband had been buried. She turned and looked each of us squarely in the face. Then she set her jaw and stared once more at the doctor.

"Ve stay," she said.

Dr. Copes patted her arm and strode off the porch, his short legs taking long strides as he muttered to himself, "Stubborn bullheaded Swedes! What can you do with 'em?"

The next six years seemed to kaleidoscope through my memory.

I remembered my brother Nels going off to college twenty miles to Fergus Falls. It seemed as though he was going halfway across the world. I remember the death of my youngest sister, Ingrid, from a ruptured appendix. I recall Mor [Mother], as being increasingly silent and weary, my sisters growing into pretty young women. I watched myself fashion a violin from a cigar box and slip away to the barn to practice. A faint smile crossed my face as I thought about standing on top of the haymow and preaching, like Pastor Stigge, to the cows.

I squeezed my eyelids tight, trying to bypass the night I had packed to leave for college, forgetting in the excitement to lock the barn door. In the morning the temperature was below zero. When I went out to milk for the last time, the cows were gone. With guilty fright I called my collie, Flika, and started off at a dead run to round up the animals so as to have them back in the barn by the time Mor got up.

I searched for several hours, trying to find the cows that had wandered deep into the woods to escape the freezing temperature. As I ran, I took great gulps of icy air. Tears came to my eyes. Each breath seemed to cut into my chest. By the time I had the cows in the barn and the milking started I could scarcely breathe. Coughing spasms took so much of my strength, I found it difficult to finish the chores.

Worried, Mor hitched up the buggy, put my clothes on the seat, and drove me to town to see the family doctor. Dr. Copes didn't see anything seriously wrong and simply told me to rest.

There was no improvement in my condition, however, only a steady weakening from the deep, hoarse cough that wracked me night and day. In the meantime I had gone to Fergus Falls to join Nels at school. Working for my board and room, studying long hours at night took their toll. Several weeks later in the schoolroom I collapsed and was taken to the St. Barnabas Hospital in Minneapolis in critical condition.

After exhaustive tests, the doctors found not only tuberculosis, but typhoid as well.

Nels called for Dr. Copes and he confirmed the diagnosis. He suggested they talk to Mor before any decision was made about my treatment.

When Mor came to town she met with Dr. Copes and some specialists. The doctors made it clear that I was in grave danger. I might not recover, and it would be better if she nursed me at home rather than pay the high cost of being cared for in a hospital.

Mor and I went home. My bed was put in the parlor so I wouldn't feel left out. Christmas came and went, but I did not improve.

One day, after a severe coughing spasm, Mor called in our minister. He suggested she contact a new sanitarium in Battle Lake, twenty-five miles away, where a new treatment for tuberculosis was being successfully tried. Afraid to wait for confirmation for a room in the sanitarium, she and John made a bed in the buggy and as soon as it was light, they tucked me in and we drove there.

It was evening when we arrived. Mor and John were ushered into an office where they met Dr. N. S. Jones, the physician in charge. I was lifted from the buggy and placed in a room. Nehemiah Jones was an extremely kind and sensitive person, his gentle nature belying his fierce appearance arising from his large hooked nose. That evening Dr. Jones found the left lung had collapsed and the right lung was badly infected. The doctor whistled as he weighed me. I had lost almost one hundred pounds. I must have looked like a skeleton. Mor and John left the sanitarium for home with the assurance that I would have everything humanly possible done for me.

The girl was back again.

Without opening my eyes, I sensed that it was the plain little Salvation Army lassie who was standing quietly at the side of my bed and not one of the nurses. Exactly how I knew it was she, I wasn't sure. Maybe it was the soft, sedate sound of her footsteps when she entered the room, very different from the brisk clip, clip of the nurses' heels. Or maybe it was the scent of the small bunch of flowers she always brought with her.

"Young man, Andrew." The girl leaned over the bed.

I pretended to be asleep. The first morning she had come I had watched her closely from the moment she entered. She was a tiny person. I guessed her to be about twenty, only a few years older than I. She was not really pretty, but her round face was honest and sympathetic.

"Good morning," she had said, her cheeks faintly flushed beneath the gray bonnet. "I'm a home missionary; I've brought you some flowers." She paused shyly and then, as if not too sure what to say, continued, "My mother grows them in a small hothouse."

I had tried to thank her but the effort started another coughing fit. The choking, whooping noise brought a nurse

who helped me use the basin. Embarrassed at my weakness
in front of a young girl and too spent to speak again, I
pulled the sheet over my head. I didn't emerge from my
white cocoon until I was sure the girl had left.

Four days had passed since her first visit. She had
visited me every morning, always bringing a small bunch
of fresh flowers which she placed in a glass beside my bed.
Each time she had come, I had feigned sleep. The decep-
tion was not difficult. I had become steadily weaker. Now
even opening my eyes was an effort. Every day before
she left, the girl had paused at the foot of the bed and bowed
her head for a moment. I thought she was praying for me
and it embarrassed me.

"Andrew." The girl spoke, this time in a louder voice
than before. "Andrew Hendricks. Please, I know you're
conscious. I want to tell you good-bye."

I opened my eyes.

She leaned toward me. "Andrew, I don't know why,
but I'm convinced you're not supposed to die."

I turned away from her toward the wall so that she
couldn't see the tears in my eyes.

"I am going to die," I said stubbornly. "Dr. Jones told
the nurse last night." I stopped, unable to say more as
sobs shook me.

The young woman looked sorrowfully at me for a few
seconds. She took a small book from a pocket of her blue
serge uniform.

"Please listen." She spoke softly but firmly. "I want
to read something very important to you. You do believe
the Bible is true, don't you, Andrew?"

I didn't answer.

She sat down on the straight-backed chair at the foot
of the bed and began to read. She read the accounts
of Jesus' miracles: how he healed the lepers, the centurian's

servant, Peter's mother-in-law, the man with the withered hand, and many others. As a final passage, she read of the raising of Lazarus from the dead.

When she had finished, she put away the little Testament and looked at me. Still I lay with my face to the wall.

Her hand touched my shoulder. "I have to go now. I am leaving for the city tomorrow to go to college. I hope to become a medical missionary." She paused, "Good-bye, Andrew."

"Good-bye," I whispered listlessly.

The girl turned and walked slowly toward the door. Suddenly, she turned. With two quick steps she reached the bedside. She grabbed me by the shoulders. Though I had lost nearly a hundred pounds in the past months, still my six-foot frame was heavy for her. With sudden strength she forced me to sit up and face her, shaking me as she did so.

"Young man, you listen to me," she commanded. "Why don't you believe that the God who has the power to heal the sick and raise the dead can make you well again?"

Startled by her intensity, I could only stare at her. "I believe God can do anything—he wants to do."

I turned away from her again. "But he doesn't want me to get well. He wants me to die like Father did."

"Have you asked him?" inquired the girl.

I shook my head.

"Oh Andrew, it's not begging to admit you need God and ask him for his help. I believe he would make you well if only you would ask him. Are you going to let your stubborn Swedish pride kill you?"

I had no reply for that.

The young woman wiped the tears from her face. She paused at the door. "I will continue to pray for you. Please Andrew, don't be stubborn; at least ask. Good-bye."

She left. I lay there all afternoon, my eyes closed. But I didn't sleep. The biblical accounts of Jesus' healing kept going through my mind. They were interwoven with what the girl had said. "If only you will ask him." The words would not leave me alone.

That evening when the nurse came with milk and lime water, I waved away the glass. "Nurse Clark, there is a little Testament my mother put in my bag. Would you please bring it to me?"

She left, taking the milk with her. I lay still for a long time, just holding the Testament in my hand. Again and again the words, "If you will ask," came to mind. Then they became more insistent. "If only you will ask, he will heal, admit your need, only ask, stubborn pride will kill you, only ask, ask, ask." In complete desperation I threw my arms upward and cried out.

"Please help me!"

My strength spent, I dropped my arms, my breath coming in tearing gasps. Slowly the exhaustion passed. I fell into a deep sleep. I had a dream. Multitudes of people were going by my bed. They were shoving and crowding toward a deep, bottomless pit. Out of this abyss came screams and moans, but the crowds appeared unaware of their peril. They continued to move forward till they too tumbled over the edge. Only then did they realize the horrors awaiting them. Their cries were hideous to hear.

Despair gripped me as I watched them and heard their cries. I attempted to call out, to warn them of their danger, but I could make no sound. I was helpless; I could not aid them in any way. Suddenly, I wakened, trembling. A thought, as though it were a voice, sounded in my head.

"Would you try to stop them if you could?"

I tossed on the pillow in anguish for a moment. Then I could hear myself saying, "Yes, yes, yes. Oh God, yes!"

The dreadful scene immediately vanished. Over my body crept a sensation of warmth. It started at my feet and rapidly spread upward, enveloping me in heat. My veins pulsed; the nagging, deadening, tubercular weight was lifted from my chest. Such a surge of strength came to me that I couldn't restrain it. It lifted me to the head of the bed where I sat on my knees. My hands reached high in the air. I was laughing and crying at the same time, overwhelmed by this joyous feeling.

The first ecstasy of happiness had passed. I was dazed. Yet here I was, sitting up for the first time in weeks. I inspected myself. My hands were thin but they were no longer shaking. I swung my legs over the side of the bed. They too were just as thin and bony as before, but I felt new strength in them.

I was sure they would hold me upright; in a few minutes I would try them. But there was something even more important: my chest. For the first time in over a year there was no nagging urge to cough. Tentatively, testingly, I cleared my throat. No paroxysm seized me. I tried again, but all I produced was a dry, hacking sound. I couldn't even start a coughing fit when I tried. I was convinced that a miracle had taken place, that God had healed me. It had not been a dream. I rubbed a hand over my chest and once more I cried, but these tears were tears of happiness and gratitude.

At this moment, the doctor, accompanied by Mor and my brother Nels, entered the room. The sight of me sitting upright, when they had expected to find me prostrate and near death, frightened them.

Mor was affected the most. She was sure she was witnessing my death agony. Although she was a strong, hardy woman, this sight was too much for her already overtaxed strength. She fainted.

For several hectic moments, the doctor had his hands full trying to restore order to my room. Shouting for a nurse to bring smelling salts, he helped Nels half-carry, half-walk Mor to a chair. Leaving her with Nels, he turned his attention to me who, he thought, must be in hysterics.

"Now, now, Andrew." His strong hands slowly but firmly forced me back beneath the blankets. "You mustn't expose yourself like this," he said in a soothing voice. "This thrashing about might start another hemorrhage. We don't want to do that, do we?"

I tried to make the kindly doctor understand what had happened.

"I'm not sick any longer. I'm all right. I'm well! Don't you understand?" I pleaded. "God made me well."

The doctor was a tall man with a slight stoop. He had reached that time of life when everything about him appeared to be gray. His thinning hair, his sharply trimmed beard, even the cutaway coat that he habitually wore, and the rubber tubes of the stethoscope which hung from one of its pockets were all varying shades of gray. It was this stethoscope which he now placed on my chest.

"Well, young man, let's see if you've managed to do yourself any damage."

"I'm not out of my mind, Doctor," I insisted. "I'm well. And I'm hungry." My last words were a shout. I was determined to make them understand.

Mor, having regained consciousness, was sitting with her face in her hands, sobbing with grief as she rocked back and forth. My strange demand for food must have convinced her even more that I was not totally irrational. The doctor, finished with his examination, turned to her.

"Please calm yourself, Madam," he said. "The boy doesn't seem to be in any immediate danger." Putting an arm around Mor, he guided her out into the corridor, motioning for Nels to follow.

A few minutes later he returned to my room, having sent the others off for a good night's sleep.

The doctor placed a thermometer in my mouth. Taking a large turnip watch out of his pocket he held it in one hand while he held my wrist with the other. Then he examined my chest and back for the second time that evening. The expression on his face was growing more and more puzzled. Finally, he turned to Nurse Clark.

"Something *has* happened to this lad," he said. "For the first time since he was admitted, he isn't having coughing spasms, and his temperature, pulse, and respiration are practically normal."

Before leaving, Dr. Jones gave Nurse Clark special instructions for the night staff regarding my treatment.

"I don't think he will need any sedation, but have him watched very closely. This is such an unusual case that anything could happen."

3

Off to California

I tried to stay awake after the doctor left. I wanted to think about everything that had happened, especially the wretched people I had seen. What did the dream mean? What was I supposed to do now? But the exertion had made me exceedingly tired and I couldn't keep my eyes open. I slept soundly until late the next morning.

A little while after I awoke the doctor arrived. He checked my pulse, temperature, and respiration. He picked up the chart and read it.

"Hmmm, I see there was no coughing during the night," he said. He turned to me and asked, "How do you feel, Son?"

"Hungry," I replied. "I'd like some fried ham and fried eggs and fried potatoes and buttered toast and coffee."

Dr. Jones made a face. "We had better eliminate the fried ham and eggs but Nurse Clark can order you some poached eggs on toast and some warm milk. What about that?"

The doctor looked out the window and fingered his stethoscope for a few minutes in silence. He seemed to be feeling for just the right words.

"Andrew, Providence has evidently done something

miraculous for you," he said. "However, we had better go slowly."

Seeing the dejected look which must have crept over my face, Dr. Jones sat on the edge of the bed and took both of my hands in his. "Son, after I left you last night I couldn't sleep. I sat in my office for hours and tried to think of something, anything, that would indicate either a natural or a medical reason for your recovery. There isn't any. I have been treating tubercular patients for over twenty-five years. Before this happened, if anyone had asked me, I would have stated definitely that I do not believe in miracles. But now I am convinced that the Almighty himself must have had a hand in what has happened to you."

The doctor's long face was solemn.

"He must have something definite in mind for you, Son, or he would never have taken such pains to make you well when you were dying. Never again will I tell him what he can or cannot do. I'm glad he's still up there taking care of things."

I wanted to tell the doctor about my strange dream; maybe he could help me understand its meaning. Before I could speak, Nurse Clark entered with the breakfast tray breaking the mood of intensity that had pervaded the room.

I barely heard Dr. Jones as I attacked the eggs with relish. I was still eating when Mor and Nels came in. Mor's face was radiant; she just stood quietly and looked at me.

"The doctor called and said you were greatly improved this morning," Nels said excitedly. "But we hardly expected to see you sitting up and eating like this."

Mor smiled and nodded her head happily. There were tears on her cheeks.

"Good for you," she said reverting to her native Swedish. "I was so afraid that you would be number three."

Dr. Jones interrupted the happy group.

"I don't want to inject a negative note into your festive mood, but I think you should realize that Andrew is a long way from being fully recovered. Before all this—ah—excitement took place yesterday, I was going to urge you to try one last recourse, which was to send him to a sanitarium in Southern California. Although he may not need to stay in a sanitarium now, I still think he should go to California if he is permanently to recover his strength."

Mor looked at Nels. Since Father's death she often put up to him decisions that she did not wish to make herself. Nels hesitated only a second.

"I have some savings," he said. "Drew will go to California."

"Hey! Wait a minute," I interjected. "Don't I have anything to say about this?"

"No, Son, you don't," replied the doctor. "I must be frank with you, Andrew. If you stay here for another winter you're likely to land right back in the hospital. I don't think we should ask a second miracle for you."

I voiced no further objections.

Mor was convinced at last that I would soon be well. Typically then, she began to worry about money, especially the expense of the room which she and Nels had rented in Battle Lake. She decided that she should return to the farm and Nels to his job in Fergus Falls. When I was ready to be released, Nels could drive over and bring me home. Never one to display emotion, she kissed me quickly on the forehead and said good-bye. Only the way in which she looked at me betrayed the depths of her love.

In the next three weeks while I was recuperating, spring came to Minnesota. There was warmth in the sunshine and the snow slowly retreated. Soon I was able to bundle up in my warm mackinaw and walk the paths of the hospital grounds, overlooking the lake. I carried my little

Testament in an inside pocket. It was then that I formed a habit which was to remain with me for life—that of reading daily some portion of Scripture.

The morning I was to be released, Nels came to drive me home. He surveyed me from head to toe. "You look a whole lot better than you did, all right. But we'll have to do something to get some fat on your bones. Dr. Jones says I can take you home for a short visit but the sooner you leave for California, the better. We ought to go. The people at the hospital are waiting to say good-bye."

We made the rounds and it was a sad, joyous occasion. With good wishes ringing in our ears, we got in the buggy and headed out to town.

It was near two o'clock when Nels stopped the horse, pulled the buggy over to one side of the road, and unwrapped the sandwiches he had packed for our lunch.

"I have tickets for you to Los Angeles, Drew." He patted his coat pocket.

Tears stung my eyelids. "You used your savings, didn't you?" Nels nodded.

"But that money was supposed to help you set up your own law office someday," I protested.

"It won't hurt me to clerk for Judge Hanson a while longer," Nels said lightly. He leaned over and gripped my knee. "The money wouldn't buy me a new brother."

"Thank you, Nels. I'll pay you back someday."

"Never mind that now. Tell me what you think you're going to do in California."

"That's just it, I'm not sure. I used to dream of being a lawyer like you, but now, I just don't know." Then, gazing out across the barren fields beyond the road, I described my dream and the promise that I had made to God. When I was finished I looked hesitantly at Nels. Did he believe me?

"I guess you think I'm crazy, don't you, Nels? Being a missionary I mean."

"No, Andrew, I surely do not. I'm only thinking that you have a greater responsibility now." Nels regarded me with grave interest. "This is only a suggestion, but I think you should enroll in college when you get out there and wait until you're sure of what you're supposed to do before you make any further plans."

He paused and then continued. "Andrew, you know how Mor prayed for Father to get well? We must realize that Father died because God said 'No.' In your case he said 'Yes.' I'm convinced there is a special reason he healed you. He wanted you to do something. It's funny," he went on, "but the thought does strike me. You know how Mother and Father always prayed that I would be a preacher?" I nodded. "Well, I think you're the one he picked."

"I . . . wish I could be sure," I said, squirming uncomfortably. "I don't think . . . I want to be a preacher. Not like Pastor Stigge; he was too sour."

Nels looked at me quizzically. "I don't think a preacher *has* to be sour," he said. "In fact, I think he should be the happiest man alive."

"If that's the case," I retorted, "how come you don't want to be one?"

Nels sighed a long sigh and shrugged his shoulders. "Just remember this, Drew," he said in a more solemn tone, "if you ever do decide to preach, I'll pay the freight."

"What do you mean?"

"I don't want to preach myself. But if you make up your mind to be a preacher, I know how stubborn you can be. Hell and high water won't stop you—right down to the point of starvation. Well, I don't want you to starve so I'll stand ready to help you when you need it." He held up a hand to forestall my objections. "One other thing.

Have you spoken to Mor about this?" I shook my head.

"Maybe it would be best to wait awhile," Nels counseled. "She thinks you're coming back here to live. It might upset her if she suspected you might not."

"Nels, you always were sensible," I chuckled. "I guess for once I'll take your advice on both counts."

"And you were always the jolly one. It's sure going to be dull without you around the farm. We'll all miss that infernal whistling."

"Hey! Speaking of the farm, we'd better hurry up and get there or Mor will be mad at us both."

The week passed quickly. I helped with the light chores and gobbled Mor's wonderful food. It was surprising how fast my strength came back. All too soon the day arrived when I had to say good-bye. We took the farm wagon into town so that the whole family could go to the depot with me, to see me off. They gathered close around me on the platform, each wanting to get in one last word.

"Don't let that education you're going to receive in California give you a swelled head," admonished Nels. "I may need to borrow that derby and I don't want it to be too big."

"I'll send it back to you, gladly," I answered. "People might take me for a politician." A whistle sounded in the distance. In a great clanging roar and cloud of steam, the train came in and stood there, the engine breathing heavily.

"All-ll aboard!" droned the conductor, consulting his heavy gold watch. Frightened that the train might leave without me, I climbed onto the first step and turned to kiss the girls, shake hands with John and Nels and give Mor a great big hug. Then I hurried to get a seat by the window. The train didn't pull out right away so I could talk to them some more. Mor was twisting her handkerchief nervously as she tried to say one last word to me.

"Don't talk to strangers, Drew. Don't lay anything down, or someone will steal it. Don't go to a fancy school that costs lots of money. But don't go to a cheap one either, but try to find one where you can learn fast. Don't . . ."

"Mother!" interrupted Anna. "You've been through all of that a hundred times. Don't you realize, Andrew's a man? He can take care of himself."

The whistle's blast drowned Mor's last warning. As the train pulled out, I remembered only the look of her eyes that glistened with unshed tears. . . .

The church was absolutely silent as Andrew finished his story. A spontaneous wave of applause broke out, bringing the congregation to its feet. Andrew lifted his head and turned to look for Fawn. The applause reached its peak, as he motioned her to come to his side. The congregation elbowed each other in the rush to congratulate their pastor on his stirring talk.

The children, with awed expressions, took it all in. They were seeing their Papa with new eyes.

4

"You Will Never Be a Stranger Again"

Seventeen-year-old Andrew Hendricks arrived in Los Angeles after a five-day trip on the coastal packet from Portland. The Spaniards gave the city its name. Seeing the snow-touched mountains to the east, the soft white-topped breakers of the Pacific to the west, and the gently rolling hills round about, they must have considered the spot fit for heavenly habitation. It was probably for that reason that they called it *El Pueblo de Nuestra Señora la Reina de Los Angeles*, meaning The Town of Our Lady, Queen of Angels.

But there was little of the angelic Lady about Los Angeles the city, in 1896. She was more nearly like a young girl made uneasy by the restless stirring of her puberty. She was reaching—reaching for space—and life. Her stretched-out arms captured the life-giving vigor of the climate, then offered her bounty generously to all. Among those who particularly benefited from her health-filled sunshine and warmth was a tall, frail Swedish boy from Minnesota.

As the trolley car speedily carried Andrew toward the center of Los Angeles, a lump grew in his throat. He tried to swallow it, but no luck. The lump seemed to get bigger and bigger while the car clanged its way closer and closer to its destination. Never in his life had he seen or even imagined such crowds of people. He put his head back and looked up at the tall, five-story buildings against the strange backdrop of mountains, then back at the streets. It was overwhelming.

Los Angeles at that time was already the trading center of the southwest. There were people, people everywhere— people of all sizes and descriptions. He saw bearded miners from the north, pigtailed Chinese pushing laundry carts, pretty ladies in open carriages, lumberjacks in red shirts and cork-soled boots, farmers hawking wagonloads of produce, Mexicans in bright serapes and wide sombreros, dandies on blooded horses, dray wagons driven by cursing teamsters, and all moving and blending in one solid river of color and noise. By the time the trolley put him down at the station, he was in a daze. He could only stand and gawk.

"It's so noisy and dirty," he said to himself, "not at all like Fergus Falls."

He was carrying not only his bag but his trunk. They banged against his knees making it even harder to cross the street which was hard enough anyway. He bought a paper and read the advertisements. One caught his eye.

"Clean, cheap rooms to respectable single men." The address indicated was that of a two-storied white house. When he pulled the door chime, a tall woman with a hawk nose and iron-gray hair opened the door.

"Yes?"

He snatched his hat off. "I came to see about a room."

"I run a very respectable place." The woman's beady eyes bored into him. "Do you smoke, drink, or keep late hours?"

He told her that he did none of these things. He assured

her that he was not only willing but able to pay in advance. She led him to a small, narrow room. It was not a pretty room, but it was clean and cheap. He was glad to have a roof over his head.

Now that he had a place to sleep, the next thing he needed was a job. For two days he scoured the city without success. Then he heard about an opening as delivery boy for a granary. The owner of the company, Mr. Jacques, was a big, gruff man who took one look at Andrew and said, "I'm sorry, young man, but I don't think you could handle horses like mine." He motioned toward the teams of huge gray Percherons stamping in the stalls.

Andrew couldn't blame him. He'd forgotten how skinny he was after his illness. "I can handle any team you've got," he said stubbornly. "Just give me a chance."

"Well, you've got a lot of brass for a country boy," replied Mr. Jacques. "Let's see if you can harness up Jiggs and Dan over there." He indicated the two horses in the end stalls.

Jiggs and Dan were thoroughbred Percherons. They were also ornery exceptions to the general rule that Percherons are gentle and even-tempered. Andrew suspected as much from the moment he noted how they rolled their eyes and laid back their ears as he approached. Firmly he slipped the harness over first one, then the other. It was a little harder getting them to take the bit. Jiggs tried to bite and the youth had to slap his soft nose. He poked Dan with a sharp piece of harness when the big gray horse crowded him against the side of the stall. Eventually Andrew backed the team smartly up to the dray, ready to haul. Then he turned to their owner with a questioning look.

Mr. Jacques stuck out a hand.

"You're hired. I'll send my little boy, Bobby, along

with you to show you the area where you'll be working. He'll also help you map out a fast route."

One Sunday a few weeks later, Andrew was walking slowly along one of the busy streets of the city. He had a room and a job but he was completely alone in a place crowded with strangers. Feeling terribly homesick, the young man decided to call on some acquaintances he had made on the way west. He got on a streetcar, but somehow missed his stop and so rode on to the end of the line. Angry at himself for his mistake, he decided to walk back to the right street.

He strolled up the avenue, trying to get up the nerve to ask a passerby for directions. He noticed people were turning to look at him. Suddenly he became crushingly aware of his long black swallow-tailed coat, tight-legged pants, high-topped shoes, and bowler hat. These were the kind of togs folks considered "Sunday-go-to-meeting" in the country. But looking down at himself, he realized they were out of place here. Embarrassed, he decided to go back to his room. Just then the wind snatched the derby from his head and sent it bumping along the cobblestones. Andrew raced after it, vowing he would send the consarned thing home to Nels the moment he was able to buy a hat to replace it.

He caught it at last, and stopped, rolling the brim along his sleeve to clean it. Just then he thought he heard music. The song, a familiar hymn, seemed to be coming from a large square wooden building. In front of it a long line of carriages and buggies extended down the street. He got up his nerve and went on in.

Just inside the door stood a tall, elderly gentleman with a long gray beard. He seized the boy's hand and shook it. Then he said, "I'm Brother Hall. What's your name, young man?"

Andrew looked at the man with surprise. "My name is Andrew Hendricks."

"You must be a stranger in town."

Andrew nodded.

"You'll never be a stranger again. Come on inside," Brother Hall said.

Before Andrew could think of an answer to that startling statement, he went on. "Have you ever heard of Doctor Bresee?"

Andrew admitted that he hadn't.

"He's a former Methodist Bishop," Brother Hall said. "He's now pastor of this congregation. What you are hearing at the moment is our closing hymn for the morning service. But tonight Doctor Bresee will have a special message for young men. Won't you come and hear him and meet some of the other young men of our congregation?"

Andrew didn't say anything for a minute. But he was so tired of staying cooped up in his lonely room that he was open to any reasonable suggestion. "Yes sir, I'll come."

"Fine," beamed Brother Hall. "The meeting starts at seven-thirty sharp. I'll be here watching for you. Don't disappoint me, will you?"

Andrew promised and left. This time when he was back in his room he found whistling came easily. Someone was interested in him. He wasn't alone any longer.

Promptly at seven that evening Andrew left for the meeting. He was so eager to get there that it was all he could do to keep from running. Brother Hall greeted him at the door with open arms, and introduced him to one of the ushers, saying, "This boy is a special friend of mine, Brother Page. Take him down front and give him a good seat."

Andrew had arrived just in time. The song leader was stepping to the platform to lead the first hymn. He had

never heard such music. The choir of over sixty voices, the
piano, the organ, and orchestra joined the congregation in
a great melody.

Andrew was familiar with lusty congregational singing in his church back home, but he'd never known instruments to be used in church services before. As he listened,
he remembered the words of a Psalm which was a favorite
of his mother's. "Praise him with the sound of the trumpet:
praise him with the psaltery and harp . . . timbrel . . .
stringed instruments and organs. Let every thing that hath
breath praise the Lord."

These people really believed in acting according to that
Psalm and he suddenly felt at one with them. As the music
continued, he realized many of the hymns were familiar to
him. It was only the gusto and the rhythm with which they
were sung that had made them sound different. He hesitated
at first to add his voice to those around him. The man next
to him extended a hymnal open to the right page and smiled
encouragingly, so he sang out.

The music stopped. Andrew's eyes focused on the man
who was approaching the pulpit. He had such a commanding presence that the minute he appeared the auditorium
became hushed and still. He was heavy-set—a big man. He
had a cherubic, round face with a fringe of white hair sur-
rounding his head. His eyes were soft with compassion as
he surveyed the audience. When he spoke, his voice was
deep and vibrant and pleasing to hear. It had the strangest,
relaxing effect on Andrew.

"My text is taken from the Book of Acts, chapter six,
verse fifteen. 'And all that sat in the council, looking steadfastly on him, saw his face as it had been the face of an
angel.' "

Eloquently, the minister's sermon sketched the life of
Stephen the Martyr. He dwelt particularly on Stephen's de-

fense before the council, of his Lord and Savior, Jesus
Christ. Right from the beginning Andrew lost himself in
the story. The image of Stephen, with his shining face,
became so real he could almost see him. He felt he was
right there in the crowd looking on, when the mob stoned
him. Doctor Bresee ended in rousing tones:

"And Stephen kneeled and cried with a loud voice,
'Lord, lay not this sin to their charge.' With these words,
he died."

The atmosphere in the auditorium was electric. Doctor
Bresee stepped out to the edge of the platform. His voice
was soft but intense.

"Will fifty young men from this audience come forward and dedicate themselves to God as Stephen did?" he
asked. "Will you do this knowing it may cost you a great
deal, even your life?"

Andrew's heart was pounding but some force greater
than himself propelled him to the foot of the platform. He
raised his eyes and murmured, "God, give me the same
courage and love that Stephen had."

He waited. Nothing happened. No flash of light be-
stowed love and courage from heaven upon him. He
glanced around, bewildered and disappointed. Doctor
Bresee must have noticed the look on his face, for the elderly
Bishop stepped down from the platform and whispered,
"What's the matter, Son?"

Andrew blushed. Hundreds of eyes were upon him.

"I don't know, sir," he answered. "Two months ago, I
was healed by a miracle of God. I want to serve him as
Stephen did. But I don't know where to begin—or how."

"I think we had better begin at the beginning," said
Doctor Bresee. He indicated a door at the side of the platform. "Go through there to my study, I'll join you after
we've finished here."

Andrew left the sanctuary and closed the door behind him.

The study was a small one, its walls generously lined with books. The flickering light from the fireplace was reflected on the rich oaken woodwork, the deep leather chairs, and the red carpet. He sat there for what seemed a long time, staring into the fire. The warmth and comfort of his surroundings put him at ease.

Doctor Bresee entered the room quietly. "Sometimes I sit here in the dark, too," he said, turning up the gaslight. "It helps a person to relax, doesn't it?"

"Yes, sir, it does."

"I often have a cup of hot chocolate after these evening meetings. Would you care to join me? You look as if you could use a little refreshment."

Skillfully and tactfully the older man drew him out. Andrew spoke haltingly, sipping the hot, thick drink. He told the doctor about the farm in Minnesota, the deaths of his father and little sister. Then, quite naturally, he talked about his own long, nearly fatal illness.

"I guess Mother had a hard time with me," he said. "She often scolded me, telling me that I was ornery, and out of step with the rest of the family."

"Well now, Andrew," the Bishop said at last, watching his face, "you mentioned something about a miracle. Just what happened in that hospital?"

Andrew related his experience and the promise he had made. "Every time I think about my sickness, I prickle all over," he said. "Tonight, when you were talking about Saint Stephen, for a moment my heart pounded like a big bass drum. Maybe those people in my dream were heathens. Do you think that means I'm supposed to be a missionary?"

Doctor Bresee folded his hands on his desk and sat silently contemplating them for a long time. Finally, he glanced up and inspected Andrew intently. "God works in strange and wondrous ways," he said reverently. "Son, it isn't often that God steps out and taps someone on the shoulder. When he does, it means there is no other way. I have been pleading with God to send me a Saint Stephen, a young man I could nurture and train. Instead, as I should have known from your name, he sent me an Andrew, the one apostle who continuously brought his brethren to Jesus.

"I believe your story and I am positive he guided you here, to this very tabernacle. Together we will pray that his plans may be made very clear to us." The doctor paused thoughtfully. "God never makes a mistake, Andrew," he went on, "but people who hurry on ahead of God often do. Eventually your path will be disclosed to you. In the meantime, we must carefully seek what he wants for your life. Can you come back every night of this week and the next and attend these special meetings?" Andrew nodded his assent. "Good," said Doctor Bresee. "When the meetings are over, meet me here in the study after the last service. We will pray and talk again at that time."

For the next two weeks Andrew went faithfully every night to the services in the big, frame tabernacle. When the last meeting was over, he and Dr. Bresee met again in the comfortable study.

"Andrew," said Doctor Bresee, "the first night you were here, you expected God to give you wisdom, love, courage, and understanding by striking you with some sort of spiritual lightning. Wisdom comes from knowledge and knowledge from the Word of God," he reasoned. "These matters take time to acquire. Are you willing to give God that time and patience?"

"Yes, sir," Andrew answered promptly. "I want to very much."

"Good. If you are patient, God will reward you with a veritable storehouse of knowledge. Now we must get down to work. Study, study, and more study is the only way to learn," the doctor admonished. "If you are free to come to my office each evening, I will prepare some study material for you and we will turn the pages of the Book together.

"I have dedicated my life to teaching young men like yourself. Today, we do not often get the chance to die for the Lord, as Stephen did, but we are continually challenged to live for him—not just somehow, Andrew, but triumphantly."

The weeks of study passed very quickly. Doctor Bresee spent many hours explaining passage after passage of the Bible. Slowly, there was kindled in Andrew's heart a great and lasting love for the wisdom of the Scriptures.

One Sunday evening, about three months after Andrew first came to the tabernacle, he sat listening as the elderly Bishop preached on the subject of love. It was a subject to which he'd never given much thought. He loved his family and his friends. But the concept of love and compassion for all of his fellowmen had never entered his mind. Rather, he had been afflicted since childhood with an ungovernable temper. If anyone disagreed with him or made him angry, he would offer to slug it out with them on the spot. Therefore, Doctor Bresee's message had special interest for him.

"There are two types of love," the doctor was saying, "the physical and metaphysical. The Greek words are *philia* and *agapé*. The physical, *philia*, we all know about. This is human love. It is the metaphysical, the *agapé*, that mystifies us. We know little about it except that it exists and that it comes from God. It is this love, this spiritual love, that turns ordinary humans into men and women capable of great self-sacrifice, such as missionaries and martyrs. It enables us to love those we ordinarily could not love, to do things that we could not do of or by ourselves. We are not born with *agapé*. It is a gift of God."

On the way home Andrew kept saying these words over and over. "All right then," he declared. "I'm going to ask God to give me this type of love."

That night, while Andrew got ready for bed, he began talking to the Lord, aloud, and praising him. Just then he happened to glance out the window. He'd forgotten to pull down the window shade. People were standing there watching as he prayed and pranced around the room waving his arms. "What am I doing?" he moaned. He jerked down the shade, turned out the light, and jumped into bed. Yanking the covers up over his head, he tried to blot out the ridiculous picture of himself absentmindedly praying in long underwear in full view of the neighbors.

Wanting to share his newfound happiness with his mother, he wrote her a glowing account of the past two months. He thought she would be as happy over his experience as he was, so he waited with anticipation for her reply. When it came, he quickly tore open the envelope.

"My poor boy," she wrote. "I fear you must have fallen into the hands of those shouting Methodists. Shun them as of the Devil. They will harm your soul. If you are still of a mind to preach, return to us. Here, at least, you can learn to be a minister instead of a maniac."

Soon after Andrew had dedicated his life to God, the church, feeling that he had a talent for preaching, licensed him to help hold meetings in missions and on street corners. Doctor Bresee did not disapprove. Nevertheless he was anxious for Andrew to be ordained as soon as possible so that he could become pastor of a church. He kept urging the boy to embark on his formal studies without delay.

That fall, in the week of his eighteenth birthday, Andrew started at a Bible college. At the end of a year, having taken and passed the college entrance examinations, he registered at the University of Southern California. Since he was eager to know the New Testament in the original, he majored in the classics. It was a stiff course, including four years of Latin and three years of Greek.

Now Andrew had to go to work again. The year in Bible school during which he had been able to devote full time to his studies, had used up the last of the savings which his brother Nels had so faithfully sent from home. The young student had to hold down two and sometimes three jobs at a time in order to make his way through school.

Andrew's afternoon job was in an exclusive millinery salon where he kept the books, made deliveries, and did the janitorial work. For all of this, he was paid the handsome sum of ten dollars a week. His employer, Miss Abigail Smyth, was a woman of about thirty. Her pleasant, rattle-brained exterior concealed a shrewd business mind. An astute judge of human nature, she was not above practices which might be considered questionable—provided they paid off. In the shop at the rear, she kept ten girls busy stitching hats of her own design. One day Andrew came across a quantity of hat boxes and stacks of labels imprinted as though they had been made in France. By attaching these labels to her hats and then placing them in the imprinted boxes, she was able to charge anywhere from ten to as much as a hundred and twenty-five dollars for her stylish "Paris hats."

This discovery disturbed him. He made up his mind to speak to Miss Abigail about it. But how could he do so without running the risk of losing the job which he so badly needed?

Late one Saturday afternoon, Miss Abigail called him into her office. She handed him a piece of paper and said off-handedly, "Andrew, I want you to get this over to the newspaper office. Please go right away or I'll miss the Sunday edition." He cleared his throat. The moment he had been waiting for had come. "I'm afraid I can't do that, Miss Abigail."

"Why not?" she asked.

"Because the church I attend does not believe in advertising in the Sunday papers."

Miss Abigail stared at him. "Whatever are you talking about?" she asked in a surprised voice.

"I am aware that there are many statements in the church manuals that unchurched people know nothing about. This is all new to me, too," Andrew said. "However, since I intend to become a minister, I've read the Methodist manual which our group has adopted as our own. It clearly states that our members are not to have any truck with a newspaper that's published on Sunday."

She was still staring at him as though she could hardly believe her ears and didn't quite know whether to laugh or cry. Since he knew from her expression that he had gone too far to retreat, he decided to speak of the other problem that had been on his mind.

"Miss Abigail," he continued, "while I am talking about such matters, I wonder if you realize that you're cheating your customers when you put French labels on your own creations." Her only response was to sputter like a wet firecracker.

"You have such beautiful hats," he said, adopting a more conciliatory tone. "It seems to me as though ladies would be happy to buy your hats with your own label in them."

Miss Abigail was now absolutely livid. "You're fired!" she screamed.

Andrew felt the blood drain from his face. "I'll leave," he replied quietly, "as soon as I'm through for the day."

"Oh no, you won't," Miss Abigail burst out. "You'll work until the week is out and I can find someone to take your place."

With a sigh of resignation, he picked up his broom and began to sweep. As his arms moved back and forth, he noticed that her eyes moved with them. Then he saw that her gaze was riveted to some pieces of paper he had pinned to his shirtsleeves.

"I see you're determined not to lose any time studying your Greek lessons. Anyway, from now on your sweeping won't have to interfere with your education," Miss Abigail said sardonically.

Andrew glanced down at one of the pieces on his right sleeve and intoned, "*Semel emissum volat irrevocabile verbum.*"

"What does that mean?" Miss Abigail asked, unable to restrain her female curiosity.

"A word once spoken, flies away, never to be called back," he read with dignity and inflection.

"Take your broom and sweep elsewhere," she snapped angrily.

Saturday came, the day he was to leave Miss Abigail's employ. Going into her office to say good-bye, he found her with her head on her desk, weeping. Holding out a telegram for him to read, she sobbed without looking up. "My baby sister, my only relative, the only one dear to me in the whole wide world. She's dying and I can't go to her because there is no one I can trust to take care of my business." Suddenly she stopped crying and looked up, her cheeks still wet with tears. "Wait a minute," she said, as though she'd had an inspiration. "Why didn't I think of it before?"

She fixed her employee with the gaze of authority and said decisively, "Andrew, you are the only person in the world I feel I can really trust. Yes, you and your Sunday-go-to-meeting conscience. If only," she pleaded, "if only you will stay and take charge of my salon while I am gone, I'll pay you double wages."

He moistened his lips trying to think of something to say.

"And what's more," she added, "you'll have a job here as long as you need one."

He swallowed hard and held out his hand. He was glad of the chance to do something to help her in her distress. He was also relieved that he wouldn't have to hunt up another job right away.

"Miss Abigail," he said earnestly, "I will treat your business as if it were mine." He hesitated a moment, and then blurted out, "That means though, that I won't put Paris labels on your hats or pack them in Paris boxes."

Miss Abigail looked thoughtful. "The moment I get back," she said, "I shall order some perfectly exotic boxes of my own. Meanwhile, you can use the boxes stored on the top shelf in the basement. They're not very pretty but at least there aren't French labels on those."

Miss Abigail was gone for three months. He enjoyed being in charge. Somewhere, some French Huguenot ancestor must have bequeathed him a hitherto undiscovered sense of color and line. Miss Abigail returned at last. Her sister had recovered. When she found her sales up and her trial balance not only in order, but showing a nice upturn, she was greatly pleased.

With wages from the salon and from early morning and late evening deliveries, Andrew was now earning twenty-five dollars a week. It sounded like a lot, but it still wasn't enough to keep him in school and send money home at the same time. He thought he ought to be paying Nels back, so he got a night job shoveling coal. At about the same time the University asked him to monitor in the study hall four periods a day. This job was ideal because he could also study at the same time.

Through the four years of college he kept all three jobs. It was lucky he had a tough Swedish constitution, because between his work and his studies he had only four hours a night left for sleep.

Despite the heavy work and study schedule, he continued to be active in work at the church. All this time he was also receiving spiritual guidance and practical pastoral training from Doctor Bresee. The Bishop's sons had chosen to enter the medical field. This pleased him, but he had hoped that one son would take his place in the ministry. Since this was not to be, he was content with Andrew. He treated the boy as his godson and used to say that he wanted Andrew to take over the leadership of his church when he was ready to step down. A bond formed between them, a closeness too often missing in ordinary father-and-son relationships.

Meanwhile, Doctor Bresee, his sermon on Stephen the Martyr having inspired many young men to service, had organized them into a group which he called the Brotherhood of Saint Stephen. Andrew lost no time in joining. The young men took as their motto the text from First Timothy 4:12, "Let no man despise thy youth."

The Brotherhood grew rapidly. The youths were full of vitality and they had so much fun that many others, who had come to one meeting out of curiosity, soon became regular members. Having discovered how many times the Bible uses the word "joy," they took it as their trademark. Such genuine happiness was contagious. It wasn't long before the group had over a thousand active young men, bent on following Stephen's example.

The growth of the Brotherhood had added to the increasing church attendance and soon the congregation outgrew the tabernacle. The church was not yet incorporated, but the membership raised the funds and started putting up a new church at the corner of Sixth and Wall Streets in downtown Los Angeles. It was a big building, a block long and half a block wide, faced with beige stucco. Large shade trees filtered the sunlight that streamed through stained glass windows. Inside, a large platform stretched across the entire front; below it was the orchestra pit, and above it, the choir loft. A horseshoe balcony increased the seating capacity to well over four thousand. At the dedication service, Doctor Bresee sat flanked on either side by the faculty of U.S.C. Other notables filled the platform and in the audience were several delegations from churches interested in affiliating with the Nazarene movement. The sanctuary was filled to capacity.

Andrew was asked to deliver the invocation. It was his first public prayer before a church congregation. A year before he would have been tongue-tied in front of an audience. Since his conversion, however, his bashfulness had disappeared. He felt that the ancient flame which Saint Paul had passed on to Martin Luther, who then had passed it on to John Wesley, was in his hands.

5

"Fawn" the Girl

One evening shortly after the move to the bigger building, Andrew, on his way to a meeting of the Brotherhood,
passed a Salvation Army band just as they were unlimber-
ing their instruments and setting up music stands on a street
corner. Soon, a crowd gathered, attracted by the music and
he was hemmed in. He turned to force his way through,
when he heard a girl singing. The clear lyric soprano was
so arrestingly beautiful that he swung around to get a look
at its owner. There, standing framed in the warm glow of
the street light, was a little Salvation Army lassie. She was
singing an old Scottish hymn in a voice that was both
hauntingly sweet and pure of tone. She accompanied herself on a guitar.

Although Andrew had never laid eyes on her before, he
knew this had to be Fawn Galbraith, the Army girl whom
the young men of the Brotherhood often described with approving enthusiasm. He took one look and agreed with
them wholeheartedly. In all his life, he had never seen anyone lovelier. His eyes lingered on her hair, which hung in
luxurious black profusion from beneath her Army bonnet,
down to her tiny waist.

"Her face is fully as beautiful as they said," he thought

delightedly, "but her hair—why, it's, it's glorious." He listened while she finished her song. It astounded him that this slip of a girl could have a voice of such depth and range.

A man in the troupe recognized him as a young preacher of the Brotherhood of Saint Stephen and asked him to say a few words. Andrew was suddenly glad his church had recently aligned itself with the Salvation Army.

While Andrew was speaking, his attention was drawn to someone standing in the shadows at the edge of the crowd. He was a tall, darkly handsome man of middle age whose elegant clothing was slightly mussed and soiled. He was staring intently at Fawn. The service came to a close; the band members picked up their instruments and started down the street. The man quickly turned his back to them, pretending to look into a vacant store window. Then he took a flask from inside his coat and lifted it to his mouth. Andrew dismissed the man as a casual vagrant. He was much more interested in Fawn's retreating figure. He yielded to the desire to follow her. He became conscious that the dark man was also following, walking uncertainly.

When the group came to the foot of Sixth Street, they halted, set up their stands, and opened their hymnbooks. The girl sat down at the little portable organ and struck out the opening bars of "The Old Rugged Cross." In mid-passage, she stopped, her attention riveted by something she had seen. Then, sobbing, she ran blindly through the crowd. She reached the tall man, threw her arms around him, and cried, "Father! Father!"

The man bent over, his arms encircled her and he patted her, making incoherent sounds of comfort. Her bonnet had fallen back. He covered her glossy curls with gentle kisses. Suddenly she pulled away and ran up the street.

The grief that Andrew had seen on the young girl's

face touched him. He wanted to help her. Picking up her guitar he walked over to the man, who had remained behind, looking slightly bewildered.

"Sir, since you seem to be Miss Galbraith's father, would you tell me where she lives? I'd like to return her guitar to her."

"Henri Galbraith, at your service, sir," the man said, making a sweeping theatrical bow. He reached for Andrew's arm. "I will take thee to her, my fine laddie."

Henri quoted Shakespeare as they walked along. All the way to Fawn's house, he regaled Andrew with booming snatches and even full scenes from the Bard in which he was letter-perfect. Henri gesticulated dramatically as he recited. Andrew was surprised at his erudition, but his performance embarrassed the boy. He was sure his deep voice could be heard for blocks, and that all of Los Angeles was watching.

After a while they stopped in front of a large white frame house. Tacked on one of the front pillars, under the porch lamp, was a sign reading, "Rooms for Rent."

"This is my wife's abode. She left my protection some time ago," said Henri. "Now I must depart before she finds me. She's got a powerful temper for such a little kitten." With a flourish he tipped his hat, turned, and carefully measuring each step, walked away.

Andrew stared after him, wondering how such a man could be Fawn's father. Then he slowly climbed the front steps and pulled the doorbell. A small, dark-eyed, young-looking woman opened the door. Her eyes were reddened as though from recent tears.

"Good evening, Ma'am. May I see Miss Galbraith?" he extended the guitar shyly.

"Oh, thank you," the woman replied. "I'm Fawn's mother. I know she will be glad you brought it." She backed away from the doorway. "Just leave it here on the hall table, if you will. Fawn came home quite distraught. She has gone to bed and has asked me not to disturb her. However, I will tell her of your kindness. Perhaps you will find it possible to call again. I am sure she will want to thank you in person."

Without uttering another word Andrew backed away. The door was gently closed. He kept on backing until he almost fell down the steps. The sign, reading "Rooms for Rent," caught his glance.

"Why, if I moved here," he thought, "I could see her every day."

The next morning, he hesitantly told his landlady that he planned to move to Katherine Galbraith's boarding house. Mrs. Mason had grown very fond of him. But she had heard of Katherine Galbraith's attractive daughter and she understood.

"Why, it's perfectly all right, Andrew," she said amiably. "Miss Galbraith hasn't had it easy—maybe you can help her some." Andrew was glad that he was leaving with her blessing.

Two happy, busy years came and went. For Andrew it was enough to work, study, and be near Fawn. Sometimes he saw her only at mealtime. Or now and then he'd catch a glimpse of her on a street corner singing and playing in the Salvation Army band. He soon learned that she was younger even than he had thought. She had not yet reached fifteen when he first saw her singing under the street lamp. Now she was seventeen, poised, and mature beyond her years, with a love of beauty which made her cherish the smallest roadside daisy. Everything she said, every move she made seemed to him touched with grace. His feeling for her, nourished in secret, was growing into love.

In time, Fawn became the soloist at the Nazarene church. Eventually, she and her mother joined the church and became active in "Company E," the women's and girls' group, which worked closely with the Brotherhood of Saint Stephen, and gave him more opportunities to be near Fawn. On Sunday mornings he sat in the audience, listening with rapt expression to her singing, while his fancy soared.

He entered his senior year, still holding down three jobs and keeping a full academic schedule. He had little time to see Fawn now, except at church. But she was almost never out of his thoughts. Then one day an incident occurred which brought his love for her out in the open.

Fawn had taken a job as a switchboard operator after school hours. She needed the money for her voice and piano lessons. In a few months, she was made night supervisor. One evening she was on the board relieving an operator when a thunderstorm struck. A bolt of lightning hit a transformer, coming down into the switchboard with such power that it tore the board to rubble and knocked Fawn across the room. Rescue workers found her unconscious. A doctor was summoned and she was taken away in an ambulance.

Andrew was making deliveries when he heard the news of Fawn's accident. Whipping up the horses, he rushed home and bolted through the front door, practically knocking Katherine down.

"Is Fawn all right?"

Katherine put her hand on his arm and smiled soothingly. "You don't need to worry, Andrew," she said. "The answer is Yes. Dr. Williams has just examined her. But she will need rest and quiet for some time. Come into the kitchen. I think we both could use some coffee."

Katherine poured two large, steaming cups. "Young man," she said, after a moment's silence, "I've known for some time that you were in love with Fawn. You've been wearing your heart on your sleeve."

He started to say something but she stopped him. "Wait," she said. "When I first suspected this I made some inquiries about you. To my relief, I found no one had anything bad to say about you. But please, Andrew, remember that Fawn is still young. I want your promise that there will be no talk of 'future' plans between you without my knowledge."

Andrew got up and took Katherine's hand. "Mrs. Galbraith, I give you my solemn promise."

"Thank you," Katherine looked at her watch and jumped to her feet. In a moment her mood had changed, becoming almost gay. "The sedative should be worn off by now," she said. "Fawn is probably awake. You may take some pudding in to her."

He stood by Fawn's bedside looking down at her. Her long curls lay across the pillow. He sat down on a chair and picked up the sleeping girl's hand. After a few moments, Fawn opened her eyes. She looked at him wonderingly, then around the room.

"Why am I here? What happened?"

"Your switchboard was struck by lightning," he explained. "But you'll be all right; the doctor has given you a sedative to keep you quiet. Your mother said that I might stay with you for a little bit. Do you mind?" He quickly started feeding her the pudding, afraid she might object.

But Fawn shook her head. "No, I don't mind, Andrew. I've been having terrible nightmares. It would be nice to have company. Where is Mother?"

"I think I hear her bringing your tray right now." He gave Fawn another spoonful. "Just one more bite and you're finished." Then he added, "Your mother has her hands full. Would you mind if I sit by your bedside while I do my studying? Then she won't have to pop in and look at you every few moments. Perhaps you should sleep again; you had a pretty bad shock. It might take quite a bit of rest to get you back to normal."

All evening, he tried to concentrate on his studies, but

he couldn't. He couldn't keep from thinking about Fawn.

Now that Katherine knew and approved of his love for her daughter, he thought the time had come to initiate his campaign. The next Sunday morning he asked Katherine for permission to take her daughter to church, and Katherine agreed. From that time on the young couple appeared regularly every Sunday together.

Soon after this, three boisterous young men moved into Katherine's boarding house. They began to pay loud and lively court to Fawn. And there went Andrew's peace of mind. It became harder and harder for him to see her alone or to take her to church or anywhere else. The young trio was overwhelming her with attention, flowers, and elaborate compliments. Andrew began to have many long conversations with the Lord concerning Fawn.

These little talks always ended the same way: "Please, please, Lord, help me to win her."

The more he saw of the attentiveness of the three young men and the more he thought of Fawn, the more anxious he became. He wanted so much to make sure of her feelings toward him. One morning he watched for his opportunity and caught Katherine alone in the kitchen.

He went in nervously, turning his cap around and around in his hands.

"What's bothering you, Andrew? You seem distracted about something."

He looked at the floor, feeling his face turn red. Finally he blurted out, "I want to ask Fawn to marry me."

Katherine was working at the sink. Her hands dripped water on the floor as she brushed an arm across her eyes and turned to him.

"Well," she said, "I had expected you to ask me that someday. But right now it has taken me by surprise."

She reached for a towel and wiped her hands.

"Andrew," she said thoughtfully, "you know that during the more than two and a half years that you've boarded with me, I've grown fond of you. In fact, you are the one man I would pick out of the whole world for my little girl to marry." She paused. "But before I give my consent, there are some things about our family's past that I want you to know." She motioned for him to sit down.

Katherine remained standing, slowly walking up and down as she continued. "It's not a pretty story, but I think you should hear it.

"I don't know whether Fawn has told you, but I was the only daughter of a well-to-do cotton planter in South Carolina, Phillip Marley. I came along after five sons. I was pampered by my parents, hovered over by my brothers, and once in a great while, lightly spanked by my mammy. My father worshiped me and expected me to be perfect. Darren, my oldest brother, indulged my slightest wish. It was an idyllic childhood. As I grew up I developed a disposition which was sweet and ladylike so long as things were going my way. But I could become stubbornly willful whenever I didn't get what I wanted.

"I was fifteen when a traveling Shakespearian Chatauqua troupe came to Raleigh. I pestered my father till he let Darren take me. One of the actors was a handsome young Scot—Henri Galbraith." At this point Katherine's eyes became slightly dreamy. "I went to the performance every night and I was sure the young tenor was singing directly to me. The upshot was that I fell in love with him. He would run around, still in makeup, and be waiting for me when I came out the door. We began meeting on the sly.

"Remember, I was always used to having everything I wanted. Now I wanted him. With Darren's help, the last night of the Chatauqua, we eloped. We were married by the justice of the peace in a hasty ceremony in a grubby little office in a grubby little town across the state line. But to me, it was all heavenly."

Katherine gripped the back of the chair. "My father was furious when he found out. He forbade my mother or brothers to communicate with me in any way. When they didn't answer my letters, I wrote to a family friend who lived nearby."

Her hands were white on the back of the chair, but she did not stop. "The letter I got back from her hurt me deeply. My family was desolate; my name was not allowed to be spoken. My mother had taken to her bed. But my father—my father was the worst. He had actually put a gravestone in his rose garden. On it was carved, 'Katherine Mavourneen, Born 1879 Died 1894.' Andrew, my father had buried me there!"

Katherine walked to the window, drew aside the curtains, and looked out into the darkness as she spoke.

"Father blamed my mother. Darren wrote me that Father's animosity so aggravated her ill health that she died two years after I left. Darren had to get away from Father, and he went to Harvard to study law.

"Marriage did not turn out to be the fairy-tale existence that I thought it would be," she confessed. "Toward the end of our first year together, Henri and I came with the Chatauqua to Los Angeles. Our twins were born here. I named the girl Fawn because of her doe eyes. She was tiny and dark. Franklin, the boy, was as red-headed as my father and husky. When they were only six months old, Franklin contracted a fever and died. Poor Henri was so stricken he tried to drown his grief in drink. He couldn't seem to stop. Finally, he left us and went to Kansas City. He wrote me a long letter saying he was sorry and enclosed a check. I wrote him a very impersonal note saying, 'Come home where you belong or I shall take Fawn and join the *Folies Bergere*. I give you a fortnight to make up your mind.'

"Henri must have believed me because he came home on my seventeenth birthday.

"I had made a ruffly dance costume and I hung it in a conspicuous place. It was a childish thing to do, but I wanted to remind him that I was not completely at his mercy. That ruse must have worked because he stayed. The next two years were comparatively peaceful. Henri left the Chatauqua. He enrolled in a barber college and then opened his own tonsorial parlor." Katherine smiled as she remembered. "He was so handsome, with his dapper dress, his waxed mustache, and his lovely wavy hair, that he was a living advertisement. The parlor was an instant success. But because I was expecting another child, it soon became impossible for me to share his busy night life.

"The babies, twins, were stillborn. I almost died. When the doctor broke the news to Henri, he was devastated. With tears in his eyes, he begged my forgiveness. I knew then I still loved him, so very much. How could I not forgive him? Once again we were lovers and for a time were deliriously happy. He bought a lovely old colonial house and gave me the money to furnish it as I pleased. When our son Clyde was born, Henri celebrated the event by opening a second—and more elaborate—parlor."

Katherine sighed.

"Andrew, I was so happy. My cup truly overflowed. Henri seemed to be ready at last to settle down. We lived in the elegant manner in which I was reared. Henri took a new lease on life when he discovered that Fawn had inherited his musical abilities. Evincing a great interest in her singing, he engaged a retired opera singer to give her lessons, although she was then only eleven. When Fawn was twelve, we had twin boys. They had inherited my father's red hair; we called them Phillip and Paul. Another two years of peace and happiness passed. Henri and I joined a church; our family life was ideal."

Katherine moved away from the window and resumed pacing the floor.

"I should have known it was too perfect to last. Henri attended a tonsorial convention in San Francisco. He had invented some new machines for the barber business and they seemed to be accepted with enthusiasm. He was offered a drink in congratulation, and that led to too many more. He became so drunk that he ended up in jail. When he was released he went off on a spree that lasted six months.

"One afternoon, when I came home from town, Fawn met me, crying hysterically. I rushed into the house. All of my furnishings were gone, even the paintings and drapes were being removed by two men in overalls. An elderly gentleman, who seemed to be in charge, approached me. He informed me that on that very morning Henri had sold him all of our possessions—everything we had. Henri had said we were moving. He had requested the man to give me the money from the sale. Then he handed me a letter. It was all I could do to keep my chin up. I accepted the money and the letter. With all the poise at my command, I gathered up the crying children and left the house.

"Henri, it developed, had lost everything—including the house—in a poker game. He had even leased his business to a family friend; Mr. Ruskin, who would pay me the rent, informed me that Henri had left for New York to join his old theatrical group.

"I refused to accept any monthly payments. I felt I had to free myself and strike out on my own. I searched until I found a large furnished house for rent—this one. I planned to take in boarders.

"The morning after we moved in, I started divorce proceedings, despite Fawn's tearful objections. Not long after that I welcomed my first boarders—Salvation Army people.

They were wonderful to me. Fawn became a member of their band and their soloist.

"When we had been well fixed financially, I had worked one day a week as a volunteer in the children's ward at the hospital. I liked hospitals. Swallowing my pride, I borrowed the money to hire a housekeeper and entered nurses' training.

"Two years ago I had a letter from Henri. He had made a fresh start, something to do with moving pictures. He advised me that he would be in Los Angeles, to look over some locations for his company, and would like to see me. Henri must have been afraid to face me, so he stopped at some bar to fortify himself. The result was his condition the night you met him, the night he helped you bring Fawn's guitar home. You saw how—how. . . ."

Katherine wouldn't look at Andrew as she fought to keep from crying. "I can stand it for myself, but that wonderful girl has prayed for her father all of these years. She never gives up hope. You have book knowledge with your Christian faith. Right now she needs someone like you very much."

Katherine sat down and leaned her head on her hands, hiding her eyes. Then she raised her head and managed to smile.

"Enough of my troubles. Let's talk about you and Fawn. Right now, we all seem to be getting along so well. I do wish you would wait to propose to her until you graduate in June. You will be qualified then to become pastor of a church and I will never need to worry about Fawn if you and she have that security."

The tiny intense woman reached up then and patted his cheek.

"This doesn't mean you have to stop courting her. I'll even help you take on those three musketeers who've been using up so much of Fawn's time. I believe the girl adores you and I want you to be together again the way you were before they came. Just remember, you have a whole lifetime ahead of you. Right now I need Fawn. Please wait a little longer to propose, will you, Andrew?"

He picked up his empty coffee cup and flicked it with his finger, groping for the right words.

"I'm glad you told me all this, Mrs. Galbraith," he said. "I admire you more than you can imagine. Please feel that you can rely on me. I won't ask Fawn until after graduation."

That night Andrew lay awake in bed, worrying more than ever. He had to find some way to let Fawn know how deeply he cared for her without breaking his promise to Katherine. He knelt by his bed and prayed for wisdom and courage. Then he added a very special request.

"Lord, when I tell her I love her, will you, just this once, keep me from blushing?" When he rose, the perfect answer came to him. He would write a letter. Letters didn't have faces; they couldn't turn red.

The next morning he hurried right down to the college library. He pored over the letters of Robert Browning and took a lot of notes. But that was no good. He wadded them up and tossed them in the wastebasket.

"I can't do that," he thought. "It's plagiarism."

Instead he took a clean piece of paper and wrote, "Fawn, my little dear, I must tell you I love you. At this time I am not free to propose marriage to you but I am consumed with jealousy when I see my rivals, Hobart, James, and Kenneth pay court to you the way they do while I must sit in the corner and do nothing. Please have mercy on me. I cannot study; I worry so. Please give me one tiny word of encouragement. Until then, I wait with anticipation and anxiety. Always in love with you, Drew." The tips of his ears became very hot as he read the letter over.

A few nights later when he got home from school, he found a note from Fawn inviting him to a picnic. He was overjoyed and bounced around his room thinking, "She loves me. She really loves me!"

Suddenly he stopped and reread the note—twice. "Wait," he thought in a panic. "She doesn't say she loves me. Maybe she just wants to be alone with me so she can tell me in private she *doesn't* love me."

That evening he couldn't study. Every page in the book seemed to have Fawn's face imprinted on it. The rest of the week was just as bad. He stayed away from the house for fear of seeing Fawn, only returning late at night.

Five o'clock Saturday morning found him bicycling to Mr. Jacques' coalyard to borrow his rig and pair. He drove up in front of Katherine's, tied the reins in a loose knot, and full of anguish, walked to the door.

Kenneth, one of the musketeers, put his head out of an upstairs window and yelled, "Hey, you big Swede, where do you think you're going all gussied up this early in the morning?"

Ignoring him, Andrew offered his arm to Fawn, picked up the picnic basket, and escorted her down the walk. He handed her into the buggy and climbed in after her.

By this time Hobart and James were looking out the window, too. "Hey," one of them sputtered, "where are you going with our girl?"

Seating himself beside Fawn in the wagon, he turned to look at his adversaries.

"Sorry, old man," he said, tipping his hat, "that's our secret."

It was one of those idyllic mornings for which Southern California was already becoming famous. A slight breeze was blowing in off the ocean and the air was fresh and cool. Along about eleven o'clock, Andrew pointed at the picnic basket which they'd left up above the waterline.

"I'm about to starve to death," he said. "When do we eat?"

"Right now, I'll race you to the food."

They ate their fill of fried chicken, not to mention potato salad and the other good things. Then Andrew lay back on the sand, his hat over his face.

Finally, Fawn said, "Didn't you have something to say to me, Drew?"

He squirmed and pushed his toes deeper into the sand.

Fawn began to count on her fingers. "Of course I could ask the same question of Kenneth, James, and Ho. . ."

"Stop that!" He grabbed her and held her. "I'm not sure how you feel, but I love you. I love you, I *agapé* you, I *philia* you, forever and ever, and ever." Fawn backed away and stared at him in perplexity. "Andrew—what on earth are you trying to say to me?" Quickly he explained.

Then she laughed, leaned against him, and smiled happily. "Oh, Andrew, I've waited so long to hear you say that, even if half of it was in Greek."

Ever since Andrew had come to Los Angeles he had washed, ironed, and mended all his own clothes. One Saturday afternoon he was sitting in his room sewing, listening to Fawn practicing downstairs. There was a tear in his best shirt he had to mend, but this presented no problem. He simply cut off the tail and used a piece of it to patch the hole. Then he had to replace the shirttail, so he sewed on half of a flour sack. His mother had tucked it into his trunk because it would make such a good dish towel. He was especially careful with his sewing since tomorrow morning a fund-raising campaign was going to be launched to pay off the mortgage on the new church and Doctor Bresee had asked him to preside.

Sunday came and the service began. The orchestra and

organ struck up "Marching to Zion" in a fast tempo. The congregation marched, pew by pew, down the aisle to the altar, dropped their contributions in a basket, and then returned to their seats. Excitement mounted with each bar. By the time half of the congregation was in motion, people were waving handkerchiefs or wiping their eyes. Andrew, as master of ceremonies, did both. He was firmly convinced the Lord loves a cheerful giver and he became so cheerful at the response of the congregation that his shirttail divorced the seat of his underwear. It crept out over his belt and hung down outside of his pants. The more he waved, the harder his shirttail flapped. As it danced it advertised, in bold red and black letters, a popular brand of flour.

That evening, after dinner, Katherine summoned Andrew into the kitchen.

"Andrew, I am certain there can never be another young man like you in this whole world." Looking at him with a smile she said, "I'm convinced you need Fawn now. Whenever you want to propose, you have my blessing."

He grabbed Katherine and hugged her, practically lifting her off the floor. "You'll never regret your decision. Now I have a surprise for you," he said, holding her at arm's length. "I wanted to tell Fawn first, but since you have given me permission to propose, this will all work out together. The school board just notified me that I will graduate *magna cum laude*. This was a real surprise. What do you think about telling Fawn tonight and planning the wedding for the day after graduation?"

Katherine threw up her hands. "Andrew, that's only two weeks off! Don't you know it takes months to sew a trousseau for a bride?"

"No, I didn't but it won't kill me to wait a few months, I guess." Then he added, "If I may tell Fawn tonight."

Katherine enthusiastically gave her consent.

Andrew dashed up to his room. Standing in front of the mirror he practiced beautiful proposals. He thought he did miserably.

Later, Katherine took the children upstairs to bed, and the young couple were left alone in the parlor. Andrew lost his nerve. Just being in the same room with the girl he loved left him completely tongue-tied.

Fawn cleared her throat, and said, "Mother tells me you had a grand announcement about something or other."

Clumsily he flung himself at her feet and blurted out his proposal.

"Yes, Andrew, yes," she replied softly. "With all my heart, yes."

For the next few weeks, every moment Katherine could spare from her duty at the hospital and caring for her family and boarders, was spent at her sewing machine. She even hired a seamstress to help her. Fawn ran up to Andrew one day full of news about her trousseau. She said her wedding gown was to be of white shimmering satin, with leg-o'-mutton sleeves. The bustle fitted under the skirt, was embroidered with seed pearls, and the skirt's fullness cascaded to the floor. The wedding veil was a tiara of pearls surrounded by orange blossoms. Her going-away suit was made of navy blue wool serge, with a hint of a bustle, long tight sleeves, and an ankle-length gored skirt. A boned high-necked lace blouse complemented the suit. "Oh, Andrew," she finished breathlessly, "it's all so beautiful I can't believe it's really mine."

Andrew couldn't make sense out of the details, but she was so happy that he was pleased, too.

When Miss Abigail learned of the engagement, she suggested to Andrew that her wedding gift to Fawn should be a course of lessons in the art of millinery. "I have never seen a pastor's wife who didn't look dowdy!" she declared emphatically. "You'll be entertaining all sorts of people. She'll need a stylish hat once in a while. Besides, I've seen her standing in front of my shop for minutes on end, staring at that pink hat in the window. I can tell she has a feeling for lovely things."

The morning of his graduation, Andrew decided to give Fawn her present. It was a pendant set with one tiny diamond on a slender gold chain. Walking to Fawn's room he tapped impatiently.

She opened the door. "Why, Andrew, you're early," she said in a surprised tone.

He cleared his throat and said in his best pulpit tones, "I have come to my bride-to-be with a small token. Knowing some in the church frown on the display of jewelry, like engagement rings, I have something which can be worn where no one will know but the interested parties."

He walked over to her. "Turn your back and close your eyes." He opened the box and placed the thin chain around her neck.

Fawn opened her eyes and walked to the mirror. She pulled out the small diamond and held it in the palm of her hand. Tears came to her eyes.

"My beloved," she said tenderly, "I will wear it near my heart always, where only God can see it."

She took a small box from the top of her dresser.

"Now close your eyes, Mr. Magna Cum Laude." She took his old watch from his vest pocket, and fumbled about with the watch chain.

Andrew opened his eyes. There was a beautiful new gold watch.

"Fawn," he exclaimed, "what a wonderful surprise. I had no idea you were buying a gift for me. This must have cost far too much money; you shouldn't have done it."

"Mother and I paid for it together," she said. "Anyway

if you are going to be a preacher you have to own a reliable watch."

They were preparing to leave the house when a boy on a bicycle stopped at the curbing and ran up the walk extending a square carton. The label read, "Miss Abigail's Hats."

It was addressed to Fawn. Excitedly she pulled on the string. She closed her eyes a moment, as though making a wish, and then opened the box. There nestled in the tissue was the overwhelming pink velvet millinery creation trimmed with white ostrich plumes, which had been in the window of Miss Abigail's shop.

"Whew!" Andrew peered at the hat from behind Fawn. He took a note from the box and read, "To the bride-to-be, Love, Abigail. P.S. Tell Andrew this hat really did come from Paris."

Katherine gazed at the hat appraisingly. "Look what I inherit when you get married. No minister's wife would dare wear THAT to church. It looks too much like money!"

Fawn's arms tightened instinctively around the box. Then she decided to ignore her mother's comment and sighed ecstatically. "I've daydreamed for weeks about this hat, this beautiful pink hat. It's my favorite color," she said apologetically to Andrew. "Why, it's almost a sin to want a hat so badly when I know I shouldn't have it." But she managed to look unrepentant as she said this.

"I'll stand up in the pulpit and tell the congregation the hat was a gift," Andrew said heroically, if somewhat naively.

Katherine laughed, "You may realize when you're a pastor that you just don't tell the women folk in your congregation what to think about your wife's clothes."

He walked then to the rented rig parked at the curb. Suddenly, out of nowhere, a horseless carriage zoomed past.

Andrew whistled. "Mercy, look at that new automobile.

Imagine anyone ever being rich enough to buy a beauty like that, why I'll bet—I'll wager—warrant it cost at least three hundred dollars."

"I'll make you a bet it cost four hundred," Katherine challenged.

"Mother," admonished Fawn, "didn't you notice that Andrew was hunting the right Christian word for bet? If we don't really bet, we shouldn't use the word should we?"

Andrew nodded, watching his mother-in-law to be. The expression on her face clearly said that having a preacher in the family could have its drawbacks.

Fawn changed the subject immediately. She began recounting the hours, weeks, and years of work Andrew had completed to graduate with high honors.

"It isn't the degree I'm proud of, it's the knowledge. I feel I've just opened the first book to a full library. I can never get enough."

Katherine patted Fawn on the shoulder and remarked, "It looks like this is just the beginning. The person who opens that library door with this boy will have to be a pretty good librarian."

Andrew added thoughtfully, "And a pretty good listening post."

Katherine started counting on her fingers. "Sounding board, crying towel, fence mender, pianist, soloist, teacher, peacemaker, wife, mother, psychologist, nurse, bookkeeper, seamstress, cook . . ." she drew a deep breath, glancing at Fawn's dismayed expression. "Must I go on?"

"I guess I got the best of the bargain at that," Andrew replied.

6

"Whom God Hath Joined Together"

The wedding day was set for the twenty-seventh of September, Andrew's twenty-fifth birthday. This gave Katherine time to finish Fawn's trousseau and it gave the church time to prepare for the first wedding in its history.

Mrs. Knott, the head deaconess of the church, who was lovingly referred to as Mamma Knott, invited the engaged couple to a party at her home. The guest list included church dignitaries, the President of U.S.C., and several professors and their wives. Mamma Knott cornered Andrew at the height of the festivities.

"Andrew," she said, "Company E and the Order of Saint Stephen are planning to make this first wedding one to be remembered. What could be better than a wedding to christen our new sanctuary?" She looked at him inquiringly. "Do you have your best man picked out?"

"Not yet. Fawn's brothers are too young and I have so many classmates hinting for the role, I hardly know where to turn. I'm afraid I'll hurt somebody's feelings."

Mamma Knott's eyes danced mischievously. "I've got the solution. My boy Proctor is dying for the honor. He looks on you as an older brother." Andrew looked unconvinced so she added hastily, "He's so very fond of you."

"He's only fifteen," Andrew objected, "and he giggles."

"Oh, I'll take care of that," she replied, bobbing her head. "I'll tell him if he even laughs once, I'll whale the tar out of him."

"Do you think you can persuade him to put on long pants for the occasion?"

Mamma Knott beamed. "Leave that to me, young man."

It didn't occur to Andrew to ask for time off from any of his jobs on his wedding day. He was so happy he hadn't considered how hard it would be to get his hands clean. Perspiration ran down his blackened face while he shoveled coal from the bin into sacks. When he heard the five o'clock whistle, he tied the last sack and hurried towards the washroom. There he encountered Mr. Jacques, pacing outside the door, wearing a deep frown. He put a hand affectionately on the boy's shoulder.

"Andrew, Gordon is drunk again," he lamented. "There's a delivery that must go out tonight or I'll lose my contract with the Miller brothers." He let out his breath. "I know you're tired, but if you keep the team moving, you'll be back in plenty of time." Andrew's face fell and Mr. Jacques went on hurriedly. "Son, this wedding means almost as much to me as it does to you and I don't intend to be late either. I wouldn't ask you to do anything that would keep you from it. You'll make it, all right. I'll wait here for you."

That night Andrew was too happy to oppose anyone. So he dashed out to the wagon, jumped in, and whipped the team into a run.

Two hours later, he reined a very lathered pair of horses into the yard, quickly handed the outfit over to the hostler, and ran into the office where his employer was hunched over his books.

"Mr. Jacques," he gasped. "It's dark. What time is it?"

Mr. Jacques took a timepiece from his breast pocket, checked it, and jumped to his feet. "My goodness," he bellowed, "you've only got thirty minutes until your wedding."

The boy headed for his bicycle, but Mr. Jacques stopped him. "Take the horses, they're all ready to go. I'll ride the bike."

Andrew sent the team careening down the street. When the sweating horses pulled up in front of Katherine's, the young best man was pacing up and down in front. At the sight of the groom's dirty face, Proctor doubled up with laughter.

"If Fawn could only see you now," he roared.

Just then Andrew realized he had forgotten to pick up his laundry on the way home from work.

"Stop laughing, you idiot," he yelled. "Jump in and run down to Mrs. Robinson's laundry on Main Street and get my shirts while I take a bath." Andrew threw him the reins and raced into the house.

Andrew found out later the laundry was closed and Proctor had to go to Mrs. Robinson's house a few blocks away. After a hurried explanation, she sent her small son back to the laundry where the bundle was retrieved. When the best man got back, the groom was slipping into his trousers.

Just as he finished dressing, two of his ushers, James Ritter and Karl Hinchman, pounded on the door.

"Andrew, they've started the music," they yelled. "What happened?"

Proctor opened the door and tried to explain. Andrew was having trouble getting his shaking hands to button the coat properly.

Andrew and Proctor exploded out the front door and grabbed the bicycle the ushers had left at the curbing.

Proctor landed on the seat and Andrew jumped on the rack. He held his legs out sideways and off they flew, leaving the two bewildered ushers standing on the sidewalk peering after them.

"Take the buggy," Proctor shouted over his shoulder, pedaling furiously toward the church, four blocks away.

On the back of the bicycle, Andrew lurched from side to side, his legs outstretched and his coattails flapping in the wind. They dropped the cycle at the side door of the church, just as the organ music announced the arrival of the bride.

Doctor Bresee was pacing the floor of the anteroom. Andrew and Proctor burst into the room looking like frightened penguins. Without a word, the minister took the tie from Andrew's clenched fist and patiently tied it for him. He pulled a handkerchief from his pocket and patted the groom's dripping sideburns. Andrew ran a shaking finger around the inside of his tight celluloid collar.

The two ushers, gasping for breath, ran in the door. They then drew themselves up and with dignity marched out into the aisle.

"Andrew, simply remember the step we practiced and try to make it to the altar," Dr. Bresee said, giving him a gentle shove.

Andrew went through the door and gazed out on the vast audience. Proctor caught him under the arms as his legs started to buckle.

Suddenly Fawn appeared, a vision of calm loveliness gliding slowly down the aisle. Just seeing her gave him the courage to try the wedding step. It was difficult to show no emotion. His legs trembled and his new tight shoes hurt.

When they reached the altar, they turned and faced each other. Fawn smiled at him. The love in her eyes quieted his jumping nerves. The organ played the opening

bars of the "Song of Ruth," which she was to sing. Hardly
realizing it, he reached for her hand and stared into her
face as she sang.

After the ceremony, there was a reception at Katherine's. The bride and groom were toasted with punch.
Then they cut the wedding cake. Andrew paid no attention
to the wedding presents displayed around the room. But
Fawn let her eyes rest lovingly on the silver, crystal, and
china. During the reception, Mr. Jacques stationed a new
buggy, drawn by beautiful spirited horses, in the alley.

When the young couple had changed into their traveling suits to start out on their honeymoon, they stealthily
slipped out the back door to avoid Fawn's brothers and the
three musketeers and ran to the buggy. Mr. Jacques met
them. He pressed a silver dollar into Andrew's hand and
gave him a sly grin.

"They say anticipation is the wine, but participation is
the trampling of the grapes. So happy purple feet, you
two."

Fawn blushed prettily and Andrew's ears glowed. He
flicked the reins and the carriage pulled away from the
curb. As the rubber-tired wheels hummed through the dark-
ened streets, it seemed the moon was making a special
effort to cast a silken blanket on the coats of the trotting
horses.

About a block later, Andrew noticed a tall figure standing in the shadows. The man started out into the street,
hesitated, and then moved back into the dark. Fawn's eyes
were closed so she didn't see him. About fifteen minutes
later the sudden thought came to him that the man must
have been Fawn's father.

7

The Pastor

The newlyweds spent their honeymoon on Catalina Island, then came back to Katherine's. There they found a letter from Doctor Bresee saying that he wanted to see them to discuss their first assignment.

The following Saturday morning they dressed in their honeymoon best. Andrew had a new serge suit. Fawn, wearing her pink, plumed Parisian hat, looked as though she had stepped from a fashion magazine. When they entered the Bishop's little sanctuary, he rose and greeted them with affection.

"My children," he said, putting his arms around them, "marriage has put the crowning glory on your heads. You look radiant."

Fawn and Andrew exchanged covert glances and smiled. Andrew squeezed her hand.

"Andrew," said Doctor Bresee solemnly, after they were seated, "you have long known my views on education. If anyone has been close to me these last years, you have. It looks as though our dream of a highly educated ministry will have its fruition someday, beginning with you." Deep in thought, the elderly man paced the floor. "Andrew, I know of your desire to go to the mission field. But right now the church desperately needs educated pastors. It's comparatively easy to arouse interest in the heathen and the men on skid row. But what about the cultured, the educated? They need help too, you know. A man lacking in education would never be able to reach them. But you can." He stopped abruptly and faced the young man with a pleading look. "Andrew, I'd like to have you stay with us—at least until the church is well established and we have some more ministers whom we can count on—men with as much education as you have had."

Tears came to Andrew's eyes. "I owe you and this church so much—more than I can ever repay. Unless God clearly shows me otherwise, I'll be glad to stay here as long as you need me."

Silently, Doctor Bresee placed a hand on Andrew's shoulder, then turned away.

The young couple began their first pastorate in a small church a few miles from metropolitan Los Angeles.

The congregation appeared to appraise them with grave suspicion. They apparently differed from the usual picture which placed preachers paradoxically next to the angels on one hand and closely resembling church mice on the other. And even worse—Fawn was seen about town wearing millinery which some said was out of place for a minister's wife. In fact, that pink, plumed hat became the focus of their discontent.

Andrew had pastored the church only a few months when he was summoned to Los Angeles by Doctor Bresee, to be ordained. Thereafter, he could give the sacrament, marry and baptize members of his congregation.

Doctor Bresee was alone in the church study when Andrew entered. The older man must have sensed his qualms for he got up and put an arm around him for a moment.

He removed a little black skull cap which he often

wore, and put his glasses on as he led the young man down the aisle to the altar.

The sun poured through the stained glass windows. They stood alone before God, as had Eli and Samuel.

The elderly Bishop placed two large chairs before the altar. He motioned Andrew to one, settled himself in the other, and opened his Bible to the fourth chapter of First Timothy. He read quietly.

A short while later Doctor Bresee slowly closed the Bible and fixed Andrew with a compassionate glance.

"Andrew," he said, "do you firmly believe these truths —that Jesus, born of God in the flesh, came to earth to die for sinners, that all who believe in him might have everlasting life?"

"I do."

Doctor Bresee said, "Let us pray."

They knelt before the altar. Placing a hand on his pupil's head, the Bishop asked God's blessing on his life and his ministry.

When he had finished praying, the older man wiped tears from his eyes. He rose from his knees and stood over Andrew, once again laying his hands on his head.

"I ordain you a minister of the Gospel, in the name of Jesus Christ, the Son of God, Amen." He grasped the youth's hands, raised him to his feet, and kissed him on the forehead. "God bless you, my son," he said. "You are now an ordained minister of the Gospel of Jesus Christ."

The two walked back to the study and sat down. After a while, Doctor Bresee turned troubled eyes to Andrew.

"Andrew, you know how I feel about Fawn." He studied his fingers for a moment. "She is especially comely in that pink, plumed hat." He pursed his lips, raised one eyebrow, then said thoughtfully, "Son, have you had many dealings with women?"

"No, only Fawn, my mother, and my sisters."

Doctor Bresee rose to his feet and cleared his throat. "Well—ahem—women are born competitors. They don't appreciate beauty as men do, especially with respect to another woman—not to mention a preacher's wife. Fawn could make even burlap look stylish. Believe me, she's going to have trouble enough without that pink hat. That hat could start a war!"

Andrew was startled. "I'm sure she didn't intend to offend anyone," he explained hastily. "Why, don't they all know I could never afford a hat that cost over a hundred dollars? Miss Abigail gave it to her for a wedding present. How could anyone be jealous of a gift? Why, that's preposterous."

Doctor Bresee smiled indulgently. "Tell that to the women in your congregation." He sat down in his big chair with a grunt. "I often think pastor's wives have a heavier cross to bear than their husbands," he said. He looked at his watch and then stood up. "Give Fawn my condolences concerning the hat and my very warm greetings. You had better hurry, Pastor. It will be dark before you get home."

Late that night, after Andrew had described his ordination in detail to Fawn, he haltingly disclosed to her his conversation with Doctor Bresee regarding the hat. "Sweetheart," he finished, "perhaps that's part of the problems we've been having with some of our parishioners."

She listened, her color getting higher with each stumbling sentence. "It's not fair," she burst out when he had finished. "It's just not fair." She stopped when she saw his agonized expression. "Oh, Drew," she said more quietly, "I'm sorry. I know it's nothing you can help."

Then, with slow deliberation, she walked to the bedroom, took the hatbox from the top shelf of her closet, lifted the lid, and looked wistfully at the fluffy plume. She smiled ruefully and opened her trunk. Tenderly she placed the box inside along with her other mementos. Her eyes lingered on it for a moment. Then carefully she closed the lid and locked the trunk.

In November, Baby Ruth, named for the wedding song, brought fulfillment to the manse. "Sistie," as she was soon called, developed the colic. This meant a lot more work and much less sleep. But what matter—now they were a family.

8

The Man Who Paid Back a Debt

A three-day convention at the mother church in Los Angeles was drawing to a close. Doctor Bresee called Andrew into his study and outlined his dreams for a growing movement.

"Andrew," he said, "during the next few years, I want you to be a missionary—but a home missionary," he added. "In Portland, Oregon, there is at this very moment a need. I have prayed that God would send just the right young man with vision to go into that city and build a church. Together, you and Fawn can do it. Will you?"

Andrew jumped to his feet and paced the floor. "How can I refuse a man who has already made up his mind?" he said at last. "I know Fawn will miss her family, but she's with me all the way."

Portland of 1906 was a city emerging from the leisurely pace of the nineteenth century to a faster modern tempo. It straddled the Willamette River on which ferry boats still plied, although three bridges were giving them competition. The city pulsated with expansion and growth.

When the train brought the young family over the Siskiyou Range into the Willamette Valley, the windows were coated with pelting rain. In Portland they checked into the same hotel where Andrew had stayed on his first trip to Los Angeles, and was able to get the same room.

The next morning, he walked to the nearest realtor and inquired about a building to house his family and parish. After a consultation, the realtor picked up the telephone and found another agent who had "just the right place." Andrew ran all the way back to the hotel to tell Fawn. The man happened to have a fine location on Burnside Street, with living quarters in the rear, which was available at forty dollars a month. The couple bundled up Sistie and walked sixteen blocks to the address. When they reached it, they just stood there, unable to say a word.

The building was shaped like a flatiron sitting catty-corner at an intersection. Several of the windows were broken and it looked as if nobody had lived there for a long, long time. Andrew inserted the key in the lock, giving Fawn a quick sidelong glance. Her face was studiously devoid of expression. They peeked in. The smell of mildew greeted them. Andrew stepped on the creaking boards looking for a light. At that moment a bulb popped him on the forehead and swung back and forth defying him to catch it. He circled about waving his arms until he captured it and pulled the chain.

"We have electricity," he yelled gleefully. The swinging bulb cast weird shadows on the cobwebs.

The cold was penetrating. Andrew walked over to the rusty stove perched uncertainly on three wobbly legs and opened the iron door. "Praise the Lord! A guardian angel has laid a fire ready to light."

Fawn laughed helplessly and carried Sistie into the room. "Andrew, sometimes I think you'd find something to please you in hell."

He lit the fire and began inspecting their new home and church. Fawn pattered reluctantly after him.

"It's terribly dirty," she murmured as she looked into each boxy little room.

He nodded. "Yes, madam. But a little elbow grease, soap, and water will clean it up beautifully."

The next morning, armed with a bucket, soap, scrub brushes, a mop, and broom, they returned to the grimy building. Andrew rolled up his sleeves and Fawn pulled a big white dust cap over her hair. They scrubbed a small space on the floor and settled Sistie on a blanket.

"At least there are only three corners to clean," Andrew pointed to the tip end of the building. Fawn was brushing dust-laden cobwebs from a wall with the broom wrapped in a dish towel.

"Sometimes I think just living for the Lord is much harder than dying for him would be," she reflected rather sadly. Then, seeing the expression on Andrew's face, she ran over to him, stood on tiptoe, and kissed him.

They were interrupted when a stranger thrust his head into the open doorway.

"My, this is a dirty old building, isn't it?" he said, shaking his head. "What are you youngsters doing here anyway?"

They looked up to see a stocky, middle-aged man with long sideburns standing before them. He was stylishly dressed in clothes which made him look something like a dandy.

"This is our new church." Andrew walked over and extended his hand.

"What's the name?" the man questioned.

"Nazarene."

"Mine's Samuel Coleman."

Fawn giggled. "Our name is Hendricks. Nazarene is the name of the denomination of our church."

Mr. Coleman seemed to search his mind. "Never heard of it," he said with finality.

"It's a new denomination, named for Christ, the Nazarene," Andrew explained. "A former Methodist started it."

"Well now, what do you know?" Mr. Coleman chuckled. "My mother was a 'shouting Methodist.' " He looked from one to the other. "Do you shout?"

"My husband was raised a sedate Lutheran," Fawn said. "But I happen to know that he has a good pair of lungs. If the occasion arose," Fawn laughed, "I'm sure he could do some very loud shouting. However, Mr. Coleman, we are both of the opinion that if people speak quietly the Lord can still hear them just as well."

"Amen," Andrew seconded. "Do you live near here, Mr. Coleman?"

Mr. Coleman pointed through the dusty window to a place across the street. "I'm staying in that boarding house for a few weeks, visiting friends," he answered. "I've just returned from Alaska and I'm on my way home to Los Angeles."

"We'll get this cleaned up in a jiffy," Fawn was saying. "Then we'll rent some chairs and be ready for church services this Sunday. We'd be honored if you would come and bring your friends."

Mr. Coleman gave Fawn an approving glance and then smiled at her husband.

"If you will let me lend a hand and help you, I'll be glad to," he said.

Every morning, bright and early, Mr. Coleman showed up for work. He seemed to be anxious to help and soon became Fawn's constant shadow. After the cleaning was finished, he insisted that she accompany him uptown to shop for curtains and a new kitchen stove, which he purchased. Looking at the brightly colored, cheerful curtains and the shiny new stove, the young couple were torn between being thankful and hesitating about being obligated. Sam Coleman assured them he was the one who should be grateful. He looked at Fawn and beamed.

"Never had so much fun in my life," he said.

Andrew had his hands full spending both his time and their pitiful savings getting the church ready for its first service. He rented chairs and a little pump organ; he bought second-hand lumber. Finally he built a pulpit and white-washed the dirty gray walls. Fawn and Sam Coleman, meanwhile, finished cleaning and refurnishing the living quarters.

"It's almost beautiful," Fawn said, clasping her hands with delight as she surveyed their week's work. "I'm embarrassed that you spent so much money on furniture for us."

"Madam," said Sam gallantly, "it *is* beautiful, but it wasn't my money that made it so. You have a talent for getting the best out of the things that surround you."

"You've been such a great help to me," Fawn said. "I'm sure God whispered in your ear to make you open our door that day. You'll never know how dejected I was. I didn't think we could ever make this place fit to live in."

Mr. Coleman put a finger to his lips and shook his head. "Don't tell the Reverend how much it cost," he said. "It's about time I gave God some of the money I have owed him all of these years. I've always procrastinated about my tithing. Now maybe God will mark it off my books."

"I guess in order to pay you back, we will have to name our first son after you."

On Sunday morning, the drizzling rain stopped and the sun made a bashful appearance. Sam arrived ahead of time, with thirteen worshipers.

Andrew let the music play a large part in the first service, giving only a brief sermon on his favorite subject, "love." Fawn surreptitiously gazed out over the little audience while her husband spoke. The look on her face told him that she thought the audience was satisfied.

The next week, Sam called on several of his influential friends. He told such glowing tales of the petite prima donna hidden away in a dingy little chapel on Burnside Street, that the next Sunday morning the pastor and his wife were surprised to see a number of exquisitely dressed couples filling the rickety chairs in the sanctuary.

Just before Andrew began to preach, Sam tapped Fawn on the shoulder and whispered, "I've promised these people a rare treat. Will you please sing 'Jerusalem'?"

Fawn breathed a prayer for confidence. Her clear voice pealed out so joyfully, the audience was quite overwhelmed.

As each person left the sanctuary, they spoke warmly to the young couple and were especially complimentary to Fawn. One of the men was a handsomely distinguished, gray-haired gentleman with bright blue eyes.

"I'm Matthew Brand," he said. "My good friend, Sam Coleman, certainly did me a great favor by bringing me here this morning. You are an asset to the clergy, my boy. Would you and your little family dine with my wife and me at our hotel? Of course, Sam will be there. He can wait and escort you to the right place. Let us say two o'clock?"

Later, Sam watched with interest as Andrew began counting the collection to be deposited in the bank. Andrew picked up a bill and suddenly recoiled as if bitten by a snake.

"There's a hundred dollar bill in here!" he yelped.

Sam nodded. "I suggest you take that bill and open an account at Matthew Brand's bank," he said. "If I know people, this little building won't hold your congregation very long. You'll need a large church—and that takes money. Money comes from banks, you know."

"That makes good sense. I'll deposit this tomorrow morning."

A beautifully appointed table was waiting for the little

group as they entered the dining room of the Portland
Hotel. Mr. Brand stood behind a wheelchair which seated
a lovely, impeccably groomed gray-haired matron. As he
made the introductions, his wife nodded her head in their
direction.

Sam Coleman went over to her and kissed her hand.
"I have asked this young pastor's wife to sing for you this
afternoon, Sarah."

Sarah Brand whispered something to her husband. He
turned to Fawn and said apologetically, "My wife would
like to touch you. Do you mind?"

For the first time, they realized that Sarah Brand was
blind.

Wheeling Sistie back to the church at a lazy pace,
they summarized the events of the day. They sensed that
a lasting friendship had begun.

Through their efforts and Sam's connections, the bud-
ding congregation soon became a full-grown church. Sitting
down to Sunday dinner one day, Fawn and Andrew asked
a special blessing for their friend and benefactor.

"Who was that distinguished looking family in the back
row this morning?" Fawn asked.

"Their name is Hart. He's the editor of Portland's
largest newspaper. I think we shall be seeing more of
them."

Several puzzled expressions flitted across Fawn's face.
"That Mr Coleman certainly has the most unusual friends."

"He should have," Andrew answered. "Mr. Hart told
me that our friend is a top newspaper reporter and foreign
correspondent."

Fawn looked up in surprise. "He always evaded the
question when I asked him what he did for a living. I
thought he was one of the idle rich."

It came time for Sam to leave for Los Angeles, so the pastor and his wife saw him off at the train. When they returned from the depot, they sat at the kitchen table drinking hot coffee. Andrew began counting the new converts and members on his fingers. "Not only do we have nine new families, but among them are two of Portland's leading families—the Harts and the Brands. How can we ever repay Sam?"

Fawn turned slightly pink. "In a weak moment, I consented to naming our first son after him," she confessed almost inaudibly. "Do you like the name Coleman for a boy?"

"How does Coleman Bresee sound?" Her husband replied.

9

All Around the Countryside

Every Sunday found the sanctuary filled to capacity. Most of the money from the offerings went into a fund for a new church building. The pastor received two hundred dollars a year from the denomination, but this was hardly enough to support a family of three with another baby on the way. It looked as though Andrew would have to find some way to earn some extra income.

One day he saw an ad in the paper which read, "Local detective agency wishes man of good character for part-time work." He felt elated after his interview. He was sure this job was the answer to his prayers. Soon afterwards he became a plainclothes detective for three of Portland's largest department stores.

The way that he dealt with the shoplifters and thieves that he apprehended swelled the church congregation considerably. He had them paroled to himself and tried to help them straighten out their lives.

Through his parole work he gained the postmaster as a church member. Emma Russell, his wife, was a police matron who showed great interest in Andrew's efforts toward rehabilitating some of these men. The Russells soon became close friends, also.

Many were the tramps who had marked the little flatiron church for a handout. Andrew prayed with them, seeking to fill their spiritual needs. Fawn sought only to fill their stomachs.

One old tramp, called Hiccup, was a familiar sight on Burnside Street. He slept in doorways or on porches, his jug clutched to his breast.

The young couple saw so many derelicts those days, that they were on the point of becoming disenchanted with the human race. They had been torn away from their tight little world of zealots in Los Angeles and were now seeing life on its seamy side. To bolster their faith they began to study anew the Epistles of Paul. His writings were like infusions.

One night Andrew looked up from his reading. "I'm going to grind these Scriptures into my insides until they are so much a part of me that I can get through to every person I want to help. Maybe I can even cudgel old Hiccup into staying sober long enough to hear what I have to say."

Fawn's eyes narrowed. "I'm getting tired of spending our precious little money on that man," she said heatedly. "It's just too much to give, give, give all the time with no results. One of these days I'm going to lock him out."

Andrew ignored her outburst and chuckled. "I don't blame you, but I've got a feeling he'd almost be glad if we did. Then he could relax and get as drunk as he liked. If I could only get the effects of that bottle out of his veins long enough, maybe he would start looking for a real sanctuary."

"It will take a powerful lot of praying," Fawn lamented with a skeptical shake of her head.

"Oh, Mosey Poe," he laughed, "what would I ever do without you?"

"If you tell me what Mosey Poe means, perhaps you won't ever have to," Fawn replied.

"It doesn't mean anything," he said. "I just felt like calling you that."

The arrival of Coleman Bresee in June gave the pastor and his wife great joy. The baby looked like Fawn. Andrew's boasting brought the neighbors to see him. After every church service, the parishioners lined up to look at the tiny boy in a long white dress, with a big curl on top of his head. Sistie lovingly patted his face and showed off her new "budder." From then on he was called Bud.

Eighteen months later the couple had a baby girl. Andrew insisted she be named after Fawn. "Fawn Evelyn" was too much for Sistie. She rolled it around on her tongue. It always sounded like Lolly, and the nickname stuck.

This was the coldest, wettest January Portland had ever known. With two babies, Fawn rarely had more than one dry diaper at a time. Diapers were strung four deep across the kitchen. The little square cloths trailed across their heads, giving them a chilly pat on the back of the neck as they maneuvered between the dripping lines.

The daily chores, consisting of church duties, calling on new parishioners, taking care of three small children, and trying to give piano lessons while holding a baby on her lap greatly taxed Fawn's strength. When tramps continued to stop at all hours of the day or night expecting her to fix something for them to eat, that got to be a burden.

At last came a morning when everything went wrong— Sistie had a cold and was fussy, Bud was cutting teeth, and Lolly kept crying to be picked up. While Fawn was attempting to quiet them all, two bedraggled transients knocked at the door, saying that the pastor had sent them over for something to eat; Fawn fed them. In time they departed, leaving muddy footprints on Fawn's newly waxed floor. That was the last straw. She collapsed in a chair, put her head on the table, and sobbed.

Fawn tried to get control of herself, but sobs continued to wrack her and tears poured down her face. Then all three children also started crying out of fright. She sat down on the floor with them.

An insistent knocking on the front door brought no response from Fawn. The door opened and Edna Hart walked in. She saw Fawn sitting on the kitchen floor holding the baby in her arms, attempting to comfort the children, all the while sobbing herself. She looked up at Mrs. Hart, her face drawn and white.

"I can't stop," she said in desperation. "I just can't stop."

Swiftly and efficiently, Mrs. Hart took over. She sent next door and called her husband, who hurried to the church. Together they bundled Fawn up in a comforter and carried her to the surrey. Gathering up the children and some clothing, they left a note for Andrew to "come on over for dinner."

Fawn didn't appear that evening. The Harts' family doctor had given her a mild sedative and she slept the clock around. They insisted on keeping the family with them for a while. Their generosity marked the beginning of a lifelong friendship that kept both families lovingly trying to match the other's kindness, no matter how far apart they were.

Mr. Hart brought his doctor, a prominent Portland physician, to hear Andrew. The doctor brought the district attorney. The district attorney brought several members of the city counsel. Together with Matthew Brand, they gave the church a large piece of property on which a new building would be constructed someday.

The church soon outgrew the little flatiron building and it became necessary to rent a hall in order to seat the congregation. Every time the pastor paid the rent, he went through agonies of parsimony. Finally he called his new board members together and they decided the time had come to build the new church.

The plans were drawn up. The men in the congregation donated every available moment of spare time. The ladies stood by with coffee and sandwiches. Lights were strung since many of them could only work at night. Andrew gave up his police duties and labored as a carpenter from dawn until after midnight. This move meant a severe cut in their income. The little money that they had went to buy food for the three babies. For weeks, Fawn and Andrew practically lived on the left-over sandwiches and pickles which the ladies supplied to the workmen.

Fawn was excited about the new manse. It wasn't any larger than the one they had just left, but at least the rooms had four corners. Katherine had made frilly curtains and sent a box full of pillows and bedding. Andrew knew how anxious Fawn was to clean the windows and put up the curtains, so he volunteered to stay in the old place and do the washing while she scrubbed and cleaned the new one.

The pastor whistled as he stirred the diapers boiling on the stove. Bud and Lolly were napping. Sistie was sitting on the floor coloring pictures. Andrew picked up the boiler and started toward the kitchen sink. A second later, Sistie jumped up and stumbled against his legs. The pot gave a lurch, and the boiling water spilled over the side and splashed on Sistie. Andrew tore the scalding clothes off her while she screamed in pain and fright. Beside himself with grief, he grabbed her up and raced to the corner drugstore.

A small crowd gathered around, as he laid the crying child on the counter. The flesh on her right arm was hanging in strips. It had pulled off when the clothing had been removed. The druggist applied first aid. He bent over Sistie, praying aloud in his anguish; someone called a doctor. Sistie was rushed to the hospital; one of the drugstore clerks volunteered to tell Fawn and stay with her until Andrew got home.

In his excitement, he forgot all about Bud and Lolly. When the clerk took Fawn back home she found them playing church in the old sanctuary. Bud was pounding on the organ and Lolly was singing from a hymnal which she was holding upside down. The children were being loudly aided and abetted by old Hiccup.

"I sheen the com-motion down at the corner," he said unsteadily, "so I says, '*who's* lookin' out for the church?' I came" (hiccup) "up here im-mm-mediately 'n' found yer kids—so God 'n' me's lookin'" (hiccup) "out fer everbody."

Sistie's right arm was badly burned. Fawn was heart-broken when the doctor said Sistie would wear the scar for the rest of her life. "If we had a decent place to live, where the children could have another room to play in, this would never have happened," Fawn blazed out at the doctor. He clucked sympathetically. "I know how much Drew cares for us, Doctor, but he just doesn't understand. He never feels crowded the way I do, and these old tramps he's always sending home aren't ugly to him, the way they are to me."

The doctor let her talk herself out and when she saw Andrew, she said none of this to him.

The Harts took Bud and Lolly home with them for the weeks Fawn stayed at the hospital with Sistie. Twice a day Andrew walked the thirteen blocks to the Good Samaritan Hospital to see Sistie and to bring Fawn news of the parish. At night he worked on the living quarters of the new manse.

The day came when Sistie was to go home from the hospital. The Harts drove up in their surrey and took them all to their new manse. When Fawn walked into the parlor, she saw that something was different. On either side of a pie-crust table were two big leather morris chairs. She looked questioningly, first at her husband, then at the Harts.

"A present from our parishioners," Andrew said, still overwhelmed by the beautiful gift. He put Sistie down gently in one of them.

Fawn hugged Mr. and Mrs. Hart. "I'm glad the Lord has seen your devotion," she said. "I know we can never repay you. But no one will ever . . . ever take your place in our hearts."

Within a year the new church in Portland brought fulfillment and unexpected success. Andrew and Fawn could feel they were over the worst of the hurdles now. One day a telegram arrived from Doctor Bresee, saying he was coming for a visit.

On the following Sunday morning, Doctor Bresee stood in the pulpit and talked to the congregation as a loving father. He praised the work that had been done. Then he said, with sadness:

"All good things must come to an end. In this case, I am taking your pastor away from you." A gasp went up from the audience. "I need him badly to help a struggling church in Spokane, Washington," he continued. "You were privileged in having my first personally trained young man since our denomination was formed. I know you will stand by your new pastor with the same loyalty you have shown the Hendricks. You're now well established and on the way to becoming a great church. I know God will crown your efforts."

Many of the parishioners wept openly. In the course of the next few weeks, so many parties were given for Fawn and Andrew that they had to do their packing late at night.

"About the only thing I won't miss is the rain," Fawn said tearfully, waving at their friends as the train pulled out of the station. Andrew blew his nose so loudly that the children laughed. They were glad to leave the rain, too; in Spokane they heard there would be snow, lots of snow.

The church and manse in Spokane were a pleasant surprise. They were large and well-built and gleamed with coats of fresh white paint. The manse, which adjoined the church, had four bedrooms upstairs, and the downstairs was homey and attractive. Several city dignitaries were present a few days later when the congregation held a "get-acquainted" party to welcome them.

"Your reputation preceded you north, Reverend," said one of the deacons. "We got telegrams from the chief of police, the postmaster, the city editor, and a doctor telling us to give you a warm welcome—or they would take you back to Portland."

One morning Andrew brought in the mail and called up the stairs, "There's a letter from Katherine. Hurry, let's see what she has to say."

Fawn ran down two steps at a time. "Mother's letters have been pretty sly lately," she said, tearing open the envelope. "I've a sneaking hunch she and Father are courting again." Suddenly she stopped. "Mother and Father have remarried." She was so choked with emotion, she could scarcely get the words out. "Andrew, oh, Andrew, darling, this is what we have been praying for."

Later that year, Dr. Bresee notified Andrew that the work in Spokane had gone so well that he was bringing him back to California to be pastor of the church in Pasadena. The pangs of parting were eased somewhat by the fact that they were going home.

10

Evangelists and Other Problems

The manse in Pasadena was a small two-bedroom cottage on Mary Street adjoining the church. The pastor's family caused it to bulge at the seams. Fawn's impeccable housekeeping and endless church meetings held in the parlor kept her up late at night cleaning and polishing.

"We're going to have to do something about getting a larger house." Fawn's expression was firm as she went around picking up toys from the front room. "You know perfectly well," she said to Andrew, "we cannot have toys around the house when people are always showing up for counseling or weddings without our being forewarned. But the children must have a place to play. Whenever we have overnight guests, they've got to sleep on the floor. That's just not right. We'd better think about asking the board if we can rent the manse to someone else and look for a larger place."

Andrew didn't say anything. He was thinking.

"There's a beautiful large bungalow on North Chester Avenue," he said. "One of our parishioners owns it and wants to sell it. A while back he asked me to help him find a buyer. Would you like to drive over and look at it?"

"Oh! Andrew!" Fawn cried eagerly. "Could we! Right now?"

A few moments later they drove up in front of the bungalow. "Stand here and look at the way the place was planned," Andrew said. "It's shaped like a U. It's built around a courtyard and has five large bedrooms. We could use six very well, but five will do."

Fawn batted her eyes. She was trying to take in everything at once. "Someone surely put love into the building of this home—you can see it everywhere," Fawn breathed.

"Look at the big Japanese paper palm! And those tiny Cecil Brunner roses covering the pergola."

They walked around to the backyard. Andrew smiled as Fawn stood quietly by the fish pond in the center of the courtyard. She looked at the hanging ferns and the fish swimming around in a lily pond.

"Andrew!" Fawn burst out excitedly, "every room, even the bedrooms—opens out into the courtyard; imagine waking up in the morning to a sight like this. And would you look at that mammoth apricot tree! It shades the whole backyard. Why, it must be ancient. Oh, Andrew, let's try and buy this home. We can do without presents—we'll make the house one big Christmas present to the whole family." She stopped for a moment. "Can we afford it?" she inquired hestitantly.

Andrew studied Fawn's face, alive with anticipation. "We-l-l," he drawled, "it might not be too much. Mr. Hastings is so flattered that we might use it for housing the Lord's children. He has made the price almost too attractive to pass up. It would be cheaper than renting a larger home," he broke off as Fawn threw her arms around his neck.

By Christmas time they had moved into their new home. The bedrooms were filled with emoting children. They had all been given leads in the church's Christmas program, not so much on account of their acting ability as the fact that they had the loudest voices in the Sunday school.

During a rehearsal, one of the teachers said to the pastor, "I wish you hadn't stopped having children when you got to five; this script calls for fifteen. I can't imagine where we're going to get the other ten. The rest of the children speak in a monotone whisper."

Two-year-old Pidge heard this remark and made a mental note of it. When the evening of the Christmas program arrived, Pidge mounted the platform to give the introductory piece. He stood quietly for a moment sizing up the crowd, and then began in a very loud baby voice:

"The Chrithmuth bellth thound wecome, in all theah mewwy way." His hand clutched the bottom of his short pants and he started rolling up his pant leg. "Chritht wath born in Bethlehem," (the pants were now halfway up to his thigh) "and thith ith Chrithmuth Day." When he finished, everyone could see his underwear. He looked down at his bare leg. Suddenly he realized what he had done. He was so petrified, he stood staring into space for a moment. Then he ran and squatted behind a big star on the platform.

He crouched there, stricken, while the audience roared. During the rest of the program, from behind the star, the top of his head could be seen popping up and down.

The other performers, impressed by Pidge's hearty rendition, were not to be outdone. Each child happily tried to outyell the other. By the time the program was over, they were hoarse from screeching.

At the door, one of the elderly ladies in the audience told the pastor, "This is the first time I've ever heard the words in a Christmas program."

"That's because I've raised five little hog callers," he replied.

Andrew watched Fawn lose weight and some of her sparkle as she carried much of the church load while he studied. He realized he had pushed her too far and he worried about her health. After talking with Katherine, whom the children called Nana, he wrote to a hardy Swedish girl in Portland, who had been a member of his church, asking if she would help Fawn over this crisis. But he told her candidly that the pay would be low. Minnie did not reply; she came on the next train. Not only would she be near her beloved pastor's family, she thought, but serving in the Lord's vineyard. This was enough compensation. Her salary was dessert.

Through the years, Minnie's culinary fame had spread. In time, things reached a point where the women in the congregation were saying quite openly that they weren't even going to try to compete with the pastor's Swedish cook. And what was the inevitable result of this state of affairs? Every visiting dignitary was immediately put up at the preacher's house.

Minnie had been alerted one Wednesday that on the following weekend two evangelists were arriving from Texas. Fawn, Minnie, and Mrs. Brown, the laundress, all fell to and cleaned the house from attic to basement until it glistened. The boys, a potential source of disorder, were to be moved to a room on the top floor of the garage. The larder was heavily stocked in anticipation of hearty Texas appetites and intriguing and elaborate preparations were begun in the kitchen.

That night Minnie, still wearing her billowing white dust cap, from under which peeped a few wisps of blonde hair, prepared a hurried dinner. For the first time that the children could remember, Mamma, too, came to the table in a dust cap and apron. She heaved a sigh of weariness. But it turned into a snicker as she saw Andrew sitting down at the table. He was wearing an old Prince Albert coat—one that obviously had been taken from the missionary barrel. Furthermore, since he had been cleaning the garage attic, he was still so coated with dust that he looked like a chimney sweep.

Everyone looked at everybody else and burst out laughing. Just then the doorbell rang. The laughter came to an abrupt end in a gasp of consternation. Fawn and Andrew shot up from their chairs and made a dive for the swinging door leading into the kitchen.

"Minnie, answer the door," Andrew called out. "But please make our excuses. We aren't fit to be seen."

Minnie pushed a curl back under her dust cap, smoothed her apron, threw back her shoulders, and marched to the door as erect and dignified as a majordomo.

Back in the pantry, the couple had started peeling themselves like bananas. They were about half-undressed when they looked at each other and stopped. It had struck them both at the same time that they had nothing else within reach to put on. They would have to get to their bedroom which was across the yard. Andrew pushed the door open a crack and peeked out. The coast was clear. He turned around, grabbed his wife by the arm, and sped out through the kitchen. Just as they did so, Minnie came into the front room leading two long-faced, very tall men.

The preacher's underwear-clad derriere could be seen in full retreat. The man in front gave a loud cough. "Humph," he said, "I do hope we haven't disturbed the good Reverend's household by arriving two days ahead of schedule. Since this is our first big revival, we thought we oughtta come early and get the feel of the place."

A frowning Minnie helped the children remove the plates from the table and put in the leaves. Then she got busy in the kitchen. Muttering to herself, she fried more ham and eggs and hurriedly poured batter into the waffle iron.

"Yust ven ve are eating scraps dey come," she mumbled wrathfully, certain that her reputation was ruined forever. She brought the heaping plates to the table. Her fears were allayed because the guests dived right in without waiting for the host and hostess.

The pastor and his wife arrived in the dining room out of breath and full of apologies. The taller guest, whose name was Arch Parker, half rose from Andrew's chair which he was occupying at the head of the table. He acknowledged the introduction then sank back into the chair. Clearly he had no intention of giving it up. "This here's Jimmy Joe Johnson." He pointed amiably at his companion who waved a fork.

"I'm sure you gentlemen have already asked the blessing," Andrew observed genially. "But now that we're all together, I wonder if you'd mind asking it over again?"

Arch cleared his throat several times, then he began. The floodgates had opened. He began by praying for the members of his own family, who seemed to be legion, down to second cousins once removed. After he had finished with his cousins, he prayed for the missionaries of his own and allied denominations, of whom it appeared, he knew a great many by name. Then he prayed for guidance for all the officials in the government of the United States. The children were hoping he would stop with the executive branch. He went right on down, it seemed, not only through the Senate, but through the entire roster of the members of Congress.

Dinner was getting stone cold. The children were fidgety. Fawn began to worry that they might do something to disgrace the family if Arch didn't stop soon. Getting up from her chair, she slipped out into the kitchen. Urgently she whispered to Minnie to go around the house and ring the front doorbell.

Minnie laughed softly to herself as she hastened to carry out Fawn's request. But Mr. Arch prayed on. At the moment he was praying his way west. But since he had only just reached Missouri, there seemed quite a way to go.

In desperation, Andrew cleared his throat and said loudly, "Amen." Still Arch prayed on. Duck, at this point, uttered a sigh so loud that Arch opened one eye and swept the table with a glance like a searchlight. What he saw made him open the other eye, too. Andrew was passing the plates. With the prospect of food imminent, Arch now evidently had decided that enough was enough and added his hasty "Amen" to Andrew's.

At the church, the revival created something of a sensation. Arch Parker and Jimmy Joe Johnson wore their ten-gallon hats and high-heeled boots with style. They twanged a path from Genesis to Revelation, pausing on the way only long enough to compare the Walls of Jericho unfavorably to the Battle of the Alamo. They bucked their way through the Ten Commandments. They rode herd on the Devil with such hell-fire and brimstone fury that the children, no longer able to sleep at night, were haunted constantly by the specter of some small, dark sin in their closet that they hadn't openly confessed.

But the sensational approach was not exactly Andrew's cup of tea. One night, after a particularly rousing exhibition, he called the two evangelists into his study to talk things over.

"Now, gentlemen," the pastor said, "we know that the person who is growing in grace is reverently aware of the unfathomable gap between the limits of his own wisdom and the infinity of God." Arch and Jimmy Joe stared blankly at him. Andrew made two or three more false starts. Then he pulled himself together. "I fear that your—uh—somewhat loose interpretations of the Old Testament may tend to mix people up. Now if you could just confine yourselves to the Gospels . . ."

The evangelists' faces fell. "I guess we're just poor ignorant cowhands," said Arch, examining his fingernails. "In the country, where we preached most, the folks seemed to take to our carryin' on like that. I guess we made a mistake to come to a city like this here one. I guess we're just too countrified for these slickers."

Now it was Andrew's turn to be uncomfortable. "I'm sorry if I said anything to offend you. I didn't mean to hurt your feelings. But tonight, just as a favor to me, would you try to preach the simple Gospel without quite so much of a—uh—sideshow?"

"Why, sure, Reverend," both men replied at once. But in the pulpit they soon forgot their promise. The rodeo started all over again.

The children were tittering in the balcony. Bud poked Lolly. "This is the best show we've ever seen," he said happily. "But I don't think Papa likes it one bit."

Bud was right. After that night, the deacons and the board of trustees came together in emergency meeting with Andrew. All future revival meetings were summarily canceled. During the discussion one of the deacons laughed and said, "Maybe we didn't get much preaching, but we certainly have been royally entertained."

11

The Wages of Theft and Gambling

The visit of the evangelists did have one unforeseen consequence and that was in its effect on the children. They had been fascinated by the word "restitution." After listening to Arch and Jimmy Joe they were fully aware of what it meant. But they hadn't seen restitution in action, until one day they came upon a self-conscious Bud. He promptly hid something behind his back when he saw them approaching. But his cheeks bulged and some chocolate was oozing out of the corners of his mouth.

Sistie eyed him suspiciously. "You're hiding some candy. Where did you get it?"

Bud chewed the mouthful of chocolate very slowly, swallowed, and nonchalantly said, "I bought it with the money I found."

"Where?" Sistie asked with a disbelieving air.

"In a pile of leaves near Mountain Avenue."

"Show me," she demanded.

Bud started up the street with eight legs in swift pursuit. At the corner was a pile of leaves the street sweepers had gathered for their truck to pick up. The four of them shuffled the leaves every which way, hunting for pennies. There were none to be found. Bud gave the others a superior look. "I'll warrant I can find a penny or nickel in every pile of leaves from here to Kidd's Grocery."

"All right, let's see," Sistie challenged him.

Four skeptics followed along on Bud's heels. They kept their eyes glued to the pavement for fear of missing a coin. Sure enough, on each corner, they encountered a pile of leaves waiting for the city park department. In each pile, some money seemed to be magically waiting for Bud. But the hidden treasure always escaped the other children's greedy paws, even though they scattered the leaves all around and crawled about on their hands and knees. Only Duck was an unenthusiastic searcher, but the others were too excited to notice.

By the time they had progressed several blocks, their spirits lagged. They held a conference and concluded that since Bud was having all the luck, it was only fair that he stand treat. Bud magnanimously agreed. He swaggered into the corner grocery store and bought suckers for all hands. As they licked their way home, they were convinced that Bud had a special knack for finding money—a talent they both lacked and envied.

They came into the yard just as the dinner bell was ringing and hurried into the house to wash. When Papa had served the children's plates and passed them down the table, he noticed that his brood sat staring down at them without lifting a fork.

"What's happened to your appetites?" he inquired.

"We ate some candy," Lolly replied innocently.

"Where did you get candy?" Mamma asked.

Four pairs of eyes focused on Bud. He turned beet red. "We got it from *him!*" they chorused. Bud stared at his plate with watering eyes. Abruptly he pushed back his chair and made a dash for the backyard with Papa in hot pursuit. Bud circled the big apricot tree, running as fast as his legs would carry him. Around and around Bud and Papa went. It was not until Bud was winded that Papa was able to grab him by the arm.

"What made you run away from me, Son?" he asked somberly.

Bud dropped his eyes. "I guess it must have been the devil," he said in a small voice.

Andrew led him quietly into the den, while the rest of the children sat on the back steps crying. They had never enjoyed it when someone got a spanking—especially one of their own family! The tears flowed unchecked.

Duck wiped his eyes with his sleeve. "I wish we could trade places with Bud."

A chorus of groans went up. He looked at Pidge and the girls accusingly as he went on. "Well, didn't he give all of *us* some of his candy?"

That evening, with Bud confined to his room, the children sat on Sistie's bed whispering in concerned tones. They were free with dire predictions concerning the outlook for their brother's soul.

Sistie reviewed the day's events. "I wish I knew the truth about where Bud got that money. Do you suppose he stole it?"

Duck rolled his big brown eyes and nodded his head dolefully.

"*What!*" Sistie exploded.

"I saw him take the money out of Mamma's purse when she laid it on the buffet," Duck whispered softly. "I wasn't going to tell on him because I've been praying for him."

The children's eyes bugged. They looked at each other with horror. "We'd better pray a whole lot more for him. If he's stealing, he's on the very brink of hell!" said Sistie in ghoulish satisfaction. They all dropped to their knees and asked God to have mercy on their wayward brother.

Duck wrung his hands. "Just this once, Jesus, please forgive him," he implored, looking up toward heaven. "But *please*, Jesus, tell him not to ever, ever, do a thing like that again. We don't like candy that well."

Lolly got up off her knees. "*I* do!" she said vehemently.

The scorching looks she got sent her quickly back down to her knees again. Finally, as a P.S. to her prayer she said, "You knew all along I liked pickles and olives better than candy anyway, didn't you, Jesus?"

The children learned, the next morning, what it was to make restitution. Bud had to get up early and sweep the scattered leaves into neat piles in every block all the way from the manse to Kidd's Grocery. Furthermore, Bud's swimming trips were banned for a month. The children didn't think they would like making restitution very well.

At family worship that night, to make sure the lesson was learned, Papa read from the Book of Numbers. He looked at Bud with penetrating eyes as he quoted in doleful tones, " 'Be sure your sins will find you out.' "

The next evening Lolly was lying on the floor in the den studying her spelling. She looked up at Sistie and asked, "What does the word 'loquacious' mean?"

Bud, still smarting under Lolly's tattling, cupped his hand to the side of his mouth and hissed, "It means blab mouth. You should know, you telltale."

After the children had been tucked into bed, as Lolly said her prayers, Bud's sad, disgruntled face kept poking itself into her thoughts. She crept quietly out of bed and tiptoed into his room where he was sulking.

Putting a finger to her lips, she sat on the edge of his bed and remarked cajolingly, "Buddy, I didn't mean to tattle on you. I thought if Papa knew we'd had candy, he might not make us eat all of that old supper. I didn't know he would punish you. And I think he was mean. Let's run away."

Bud sat up. His eyes brightened. "They'll be sorry when they find out we're gone forever." Lolly pressed her point, "They'll cry their eyes out."

Bud thought it over for a moment. Then he jumped out of bed and whispered, "Go get dressed, Lolly, and while you're at it, bring a big bandanna. We'll need something to put spare clothes in."

Lolly tiptoed to her room, dressed hurriedly, and opened Sistie's top bureau drawer looking for a bandanna. She couldn't find one. She picked up Sistie's middy blouse that was stretched across the back of a chair, pulled the neck together, and pinned it with a safety pin. Then she quickly stuffed the blouse with her nightie, hair brush, some clean underwear and socks, and tiptoed back to Bud's room, the blouse over her shoulder like a duffel bag.

Bud gave Lolly a disgusted glare. "That doesn't look like a bandanna," he whispered. "Besides, we'll need a pole, too. Tramps always tie their bandannas to poles."

"We don't have a pole in our room." Lolly looked at her shoes.

Bud opened his closet door and pointed at the cross pole from which his clothes hung. "You have one like this, see?" He lifted the hangers off and laid some of the clothes across the back of a chair.

"Help me," he whispered to Lolly, "and don't slop them all over the floor the way you do to your things. I like to keep my clothes neat," he said crossly.

Lolly staggered under the weight of the garments Bud laid across her arms. She started to cross the room, then tripped over the hem of a coat, and fell down in a heap.

"Sh!" hissed Bud. "Do you want to spoil everything?"

"If we're going to run away, we'd better get started," Lolly whispered. Bud took her suggestion under advisement.

"It's too dark," he decided, looking out the window.

"We can't get the alarm clock because it's in Papa's room. We'll just have to sit here for a while. When it gets light, we'll sneak out and be far away before Papa gets up. Boy! I'd hate to be in his shoes when he knows we're gone and he'll never see us again."

"Yeah," Lolly yawned.

Bud tucked his clothes into the middy blouse, tying the sleeves around the pole. "I won't have to practice my violin for two hours every day, either." He made a wry face as he jerked the sleeves into a tight knot.

"Yeah," Lolly answered, rubbing her eyes.

Bud took council with himself. "Maybe I'll miss my violin. I guess I can carry that, too." He put his violin case on the foot of the bed.

"Yeah," Lolly agreed, blinking hazily at him.

"Stop saying 'Yeah.' You know Papa won't allow us to say that. Say yes."

"But we don't live here anymore and I can say anything I want to!" Lolly broke out impetuously. "I'm going to say 'golly'—and even 'bet.' I betcha I will, I betcha."

Bud looked at his sister. "Ugh, girls," he said with distaste.

"I'm going to lie down and rest . . . my . . . eyeballs, like Nana . . . does," Lolly mumbled, lying back on the bed.

"Move over," Bud said, jabbing his sister. He tumbled down beside her and murmured between yawns, "I'll set my mental alarm like Mamma does. She can wake up any time she wants, just by thinking about it before she goes to sleep."

Lolly didn't hear Bud. She was already asleep.

In the morning Andrew went into Bud's room to awaken him. He drew back in surprise. Two children were lying there asleep on top of the covers on Bud's bed. Between them, tied to the pole, was Sistie's middy blouse stuffed with their belongings. Bud's arms was thrown over his violin case. Andrew tiptoed back to his room and beckoned Fawn to follow him. "I want to show you something."

Fawn stood in Bud's open door and sighed. "Those poor babies." She looked at Andrew with moist eyes.

"Don't worry about this little episode, lover." He patted her and smiled. "I don't think I could count the times I planned to run away when I was their age. It's part of growing up. Children either conform, rebel, or retreat. Right now they're rebelling."

"Let's not ever let them know we saw them," Fawn said. "We mustn't hurt their pride."

"All right, angel, but it isn't their precious pride I'm worried about," Andrew grinned. "I'm thinking how lucky we are. If they knew we caught them asleep, think of all the precious little excuses we would have to listen to!"

One evening, several weeks later, the telephone rang. A rather perturbed voice was asking for Andrew.

"The pastor has been called to the hospital," Fawn explained. "He'll be home around nine o'clock. May I take a message?"

"Yes," said a stern voice. "This is Mr. Carstairs. I have it on very good authority, Madam, that your children are gambling. I want to hear what the Reverend has to say about *that*."

Fawn was silent for a moment while she pondered the accusation. Suddenly the answer dawned on her. She laughed.

"You may laugh all you want, Madam," the man retorted angrily, "but kindly tell the Reverend that I will be over tomorrow evening at eight sharp to get *his* explanation." The caller hung up, giving vent to his rage by banging the receiver in Fawn's ear.

"Well, really," Fawn muttered, putting down the telephone with an air of distaste. Suddenly it wasn't funny anymore.

When Andrew came home that night, Fawn waited until he had given her the details concerning their sick parishioner. Then, in a matter-of-fact voice, she told him about the appointment. "I think he wants to discuss your wicked children," she said with a straight face. "It seems they have taken up gambling."

Andrew shot her a quick glance from under his black brows. "Come on, Mosey Poe, start from the beginning."

Fawn explained to him about her hunch. "Oh, Drew," she said, "it makes me so mad sometimes the way everybody watches us. Our children aren't perfect. But I wouldn't want them to be—not even to satisfy the likes of our gentleman caller tonight."

"Well," replied Andrew lightly, "it's a good thing they're not perfect—they'd be insufferable!"

Fawn couldn't prevent a chuckle from escaping and dropped her arms helplessly. Then she and her husband planned a little strategy.

At dinner the next evening, the customary enlivening small talk was conspicuous by its absence. Fawn and Andrew seemed eager to get through the meal quickly. They wanted their brood upstairs and in bed ahead of time. They knew that if the children had any idea of what was afoot they'd be up leaning over the stair railing.

As soon as they were all quiet, Fawn went to the kitchen. Humming good-naturedly to herself, her anger dissipated, she cut generous portions of strawberry pie and topped them with whipped cream. Then she made a pot of fresh coffee and set up her silver tray with cream and sugar. Unfolding a game board she spread it out in the center of the table. Then she went to Andrew's den for a goodnight kiss and hurried upstairs to their room.

Some minutes later the doorbell notified Andrew that

his caller had arrived. The greetings which the two men exchanged were cool and formal. Andrew said later that he had trouble concentrating. All he could think of was how much Mr. Carstairs' large and aggressive nose resembled the beak of a parrot. He wondered, as Mr. Carstairs advanced, fixing him with a beady eye, whether it was going to tweak him. Without wasting any time, Mr. Carstairs launched head-on into his interrogation.

"Pastor, I am here on a serious mission," he declared. "I have been reliably informed that your children have been observed indulging in . . . ah . . . how shall I put it? Games of chance." Mr. Carstairs paused, watching Andrew's face for his reaction. Then he went on. "And I am told they were doing it for money!" Andrew looked as if he were giving the matter very serious consideration.

"I have come to you first with this nefarious tale," Mr. Carstairs continued. "I want to hear from your own lips that it is a dastardly lie."

Making appropriate interjections of mild shock and concern, the preacher meanwhile was relieving Mr. Carstairs of his coat and hat, and laying them gently across a chair. Then he began to maneuver Mr. Carstairs, still thundering, toward the living room. Andrew was muttering darkly, shaking his head and clucking, but steadfastly refusing to show any real emotion, much to Mr. Carstairs' chagrin.

Their movements led them through the dark hallway, past the brightly-lighted dining room. There, on the broad, dark table, lay the game of Pollyanna. The Pastor stopped in the door, managing to nudge Mr. Carstairs into the room ahead of him. Mr. Carstairs squinted sidelong at the game with the pieces in place beside the playing board.

"Hmmmm-m," said Andrew reflectively. "It's been many a year since I've had the pleasure of playing a child's game. Care to try one?" He looked beguilingly at Mr. Carstairs, who hesitated. "But knowing your shrewd banker's mind," Andrew added hastily, "I fear I'd be in for a trouncing."

Mr. Carstairs stood as though hypnotized. Casually his host picked up a cardboard container and shook its contents out onto the board. Out rolled four dice.

"These little cubes come with the game," Andrew went on. "I believe they're called dice. Of course the children have no idea as yet that dice are used by some for gambling." He sighed. "I suppose someday they'll find out. But by that time, I hope they'll learn that if one is determined to gamble, using dice isn't the only means to that end. Anything will do."

Mr. Carstairs peered at his minister, then at the game, then back at his minister. His forehead corrugated. "Er, so the dice are counters," Mr. Carstairs mumbled, picking up the ivories and shaking them in his hand. "All right, come on, Reverend. I'll bet . . . warrant I'll beat the socks off you."

Andrew explained how the game was played. The two grown men suddenly became little boys, each consumed with a single-minded desire—to land on his opponent's square and send him back to the starting line. As the game progressed, the mask of maturity slipped lower and lower, until both men were crooning happily to the dice, "Come on, you twosie's."

Indeed, their crooning became shouting and their shouting became so loud that eventually it awakened Sistie, who crept down the hall and sat on the top step, from where she could watch the fun.

The two men had just finished their fifth game. Andrew, as he served the coffee, was whistling happily. Mr. Carstairs' strawberry pie lay before him untouched. He was strangely silent. Suddenly the quiet was broken by a series of loud thumps, as Sistie came rolling down the stairs. The men jostled each other in their rush to see how badly she was hurt.

"Where did you come from, angel?" Andrew said, picking her up. "You were supposed to be asleep."

"I know," said Sistie, rubbing her sore spots. "But I heard Mamma saying something about somebody thinking we were gambling and it made me so mad I got up. I wanted to see who would tell a fib like that. I guess I must have fallen asleep on the stairs."

Mr. Carstairs looked contrite as he patted Sistie's head. "I made the accusation, my child. But I see now that it was very wrong of me. Next time anyone tells me such a tale, I will lose no time in setting him straight."

He looked at his watch and said it was time for him to be going. Andrew shooed Sistie back upstairs. The two men shook hands at the door. "Reverend," said Mr. Carstairs falteringly, "when it comes to apologizing, I find myself . . . well, I don't know quite what to say."

The minister's eyes lit up. He smiled broadly as he pumped Mr. Carstairs' hand. "Don't feel bad, Sir. Many times, I, too, have been at a loss for words when you did such a splendid job in getting loans for the church," he said. "Praise the Lord, we now understand each other."

12

Los Angeles

In 1917 Los Angeles was a metropolis sprawled between swank Pasadena and rural farmlands stretching to the Pacific Ocean. One could go for a hike in the Sierra Nevada mountains beyond Altadena, travel an hour westward, then enjoy a swim in the surf. It was a city of symphonies, museums, pepper trees, parks, and sunshine.

On a lovely day in early summer Fawn and Andrew were threading their way through the mélange of automobiles, horse-drawn buggies, and bicycles. They whizzed along Fair Oaks Avenue, turned the corner at the Causton Ostrich Farms in South Pasadena, and headed west on Figueroa Boulevard, which took them into the heart of Los Angeles. They were on their way to see their new church and manse—they were to pastor the mother church.

When they arrived at Sixth and Wall Streets a delegation of old friends was waiting for them. After chatting a while and renewing old acquaintances, the pastor and his wife were taken into the office. It was here, at this very desk before which Andrew now stood, that Dr. Bresee had prepared him for his ordination, where he had given him words of advice and comfort on so many occasions.

Andrew could visualize the warm brown eyes and benevolent expression as clearly as though they were before him. Reverently, he walked over to the walls which were lined with his teacher's books and ran his hands along the volumes from whose pages his mentor had derived inspiration in founding the denomination. Then he dropped to his knees in prayer, to renew his covenant with God.

Among the first to greet Andrew and Fawn was Brother Hall, the deacon who had so warmly welcomed the lonely, shy boy on that Sunday long ago when Andrew had dropped in off the street to hear Doctor Bresee preach at the old Tabernacle. It was Brother Hall who had asked for the privilege of showing the pastor and his wife their new home. While Andrew was busy cranking the Ford, the agile deacon leaped into the front seat next to Fawn and handed her an address scribbled on a slip of paper.

The car rumbled down Sixth Street onto Main and turned into a side street. Andrew consulted the slip of paper, then checked the house numbers. Satisfied that he had the right one, he pulled up to the curb. Then his eyes widened. He looked at the number, then back at the house. No, he had certainly not made any mistake. But that house! It was a huge, ramshackle structure with weary paint peeling from its sides. Shutters dangled from broken hinges. Several posts were gone from the porch railing, leaving gaps like missing teeth. A sound of woe escaped from between his compressed lips.

"My!" said Andrew, trying to maintain a courteous composure. "She's roomy, all right. If she were fixed up a little—she'd be . . ."

Brother Hall glanced at Andrew. "We thought you'd want a big place, Andrew. And big places don't come cheap. But knowing how handy you are—"

Fawn said nothing. She was trying to form words to express polite appreciation while at the same time struggling to keep from crying. Andrew stood up. He didn't stop to open the car door, but dropped one leg over the automobile to the street. Then he marched up to the sagging porch, just missing a hole in the steps. He stood there, scratching the back of his head, surveying the scene as though trying to imagine its potential.

"Something might be made of it," he said with a sigh. "I only hope I can find the time."

Brother Hall could contain himself no longer. He burst out laughing. "Did you two kids seriously think we would put you in an old dump like this?" He jumped out of the car, ran after Andrew, and pulled him down the stairs back to the Ford. "You sit in the middle this time, young fellow," he chuckled, "and let an old man show you how to drive this Tin Lizzie in the big city."

The car turned into Figueroa Boulevard and then up the new asphalt highway out Pasadena Avenue. Opposite Sycamore Grove he brought the car to a jolting stop. "See this beautiful park?"

Fawn and Andrew dutifully nodded. There was so much of it they could hardly help seeing it.

"How would you like to have this as a playground for your children?" The young couple peered at him with gratifying curiosity. "Now turn around."

They turned. There on a small knoll stood a low, wide, rambling Japanese-style residence with a red-tiled pagoda-type roof. The velvety green lawn was framed on all sides by artistic plantings and rare shrubs which provided a border as elegant as brocade on a gown.

Brother Hall let a moment of silence go by for dramatic effect. Then he announced, "Your new home."

"Ours?" Fawn gasped. Brother Hall nodded. She leaned forward and stared at him quizzically. "You aren't still teasing us, are you, Brother Hall?"

The deacon shook his head vehemently. "I never was more serious in my life."

Andrew let out his breath. "What a beauty!" he murmured.

Awestruck, they moved silently up the sidewalk to the front entrance and they found the courtyard filled with tropical plants.

"Just think," Fawn sighed rapturously. "We'll be living in a garden of Eden, practically." Then her voice rose. "Look through the glass. I see plants inside the house, too."

Andrew inserted the key into the heavy front door, stepped into the entryway, and beckoned to the others. "Come here and look."

Fawn was right on his heels. "Why," she said, "it's the most beautiful front room I've ever seen."

The soft brown walls were done in Japanese wood, which had been rubbed to a satiny finish. A black marble fireplace stood against one wall. Andirons in the form of fat Buddhas waited to hold a bright fire.

"What a perfect background for weddings!" Fawn's eyes were bright with visions of what their future life would be like in the lovely house. "The whole architecture is like frozen music," she said ecstatically.

She ran over and opened a door in the corner which led into a small room. "Oh," she exclaimed, "this would be perfect for Minnie." She closed the door and looked at Andrew with brimming eyes. "Mercy! Mercy!" was all her usually articulate husband could find to say.

Brother Hall stood there beaming.

Walking slowly across the entryway into the dining room, Fawn suddenly broke from Andrew's arm and ran over to the wainscoted walls. Tenderly she ran her fingertips over the tapestry.

"Drew! It's real—real tapestry! Look at the beautiful colors in gold and blue."

"Why, they're the royal colors of Sweden," said Andrew.

Fawn's eyes moved up to the plate railing along the top of the wainscoting. "Darling, now we can display all of our beautiful wedding china. And we can put our cut glass on the big sideboard over there." She leaned against the wall and looked dreamily around the room. "My cup runneth over. Just think what it would be like to live surrounded by such beauty."

They pushed open the double swinging doors, and found themselves in an enormous kitchen. It was such a kitchen as they never dreamed existed—all gleaming brass and wooden cabinets.

"Camphor wood," pronounced Andrew with authority. The cabinets, with brass fittings, lined three walls of the room. Smack in the center, like some pagan altar on an island, stood a huge black stove. Over it, a conical brass hood hung from the ceiling. But it was the sink and drainboards of solid marble that enthralled Fawn. She stood and stared at them, bereft of speech. Then she ran to a door which opened into a bath. The next door she investigated brought a small shriek. "Andrew! There's a screened porch that goes the *entire* width of the house."

Brother Hall's voice broke in upon them, echoing from the far end of the house. "Come look at your den!"

Hand in hand, they ran down the hall. Andrew whistled at the sight of it. The walls were wood paneled; bookcases lined two of them. He wagged his head incredulously. "Imagine having a room like this for a study."

"Wait—you haven't seen anything yet," said Brother Hall. "Now for the upstairs."

They mounted a gently curving staircase and saw before them a long, wide hall. "Six bedrooms," announced Brother Hall, with all the restrained awe of an auctioneer. "Two on one side with a bath in between, and four on the other side opening on a Romeo and Juliet balcony which runs the length of the house."

"Gracious me, sakes alive! Look at all the closet space," cried Fawn. "And dressing rooms. Why, there must be one in every bedroom. I'm so overwhelmed, I'm shaking all over. Drew! For goodness sake, *say* something!"

Andrew took a deep breath. "I'm dumbfounded."

"Andrew, I can think of you as surprised, all right," Brother Hall laughed. "But dumbfounded—never! Wait, though, until you see the orchard out in back, plus the riding stables. That just might do it."

Andrew put his arm around the deacon's shoulders. A frown gathered on his forehead. "I'm not sure we ought to accept it." He ignored his wife who was looking at him apprehensively with the pleading eyes of a spaniel. "It doesn't seem—well, in character for a humble preacher. Besides, can the church really afford it? After all my salary wouldn't pay the taxes. I don't want people to think the church is rich or that I have an outside income. Even our furniture will look pretty shabby in this place. It's far too fine for us."

Brother Hall's blue eyes danced. "Why must God's children always think they must live in shacks? I think God paved the way for the church to acquire this teitaku, or Japanese mansion if you prefer, at a terrific bargain. He knew you and Fawn would not only share it with multitudes, but glorify HIM." He squinted his eyes and went on, "I won't say we were lucky; I'd say we were blessed. The man who owned it was an importer. He built this place when he retired. He lived just long enough to see that every shrub and every tree was planted in its proper place. Upon his death, his wife moved east to be near her children.

"Doctor Paul—Doctor Bresee's son—was their family physician. When he learned you two were called to our church he thought it would be an ideal manse for you. The widow was agreeable to selling the house for a nominal fee —provided that nothing would be changed and the place would be maintained in tiptop condition. Doctor Paul assured her that if anyone knew how to care for a home, it would be you two."

His explanation seemed to satisfy Andrew, and it quieted Fawn's fears. She talked a blue streak as they drove Brother Hall home.

Several weeks later the family moved in. The first thing Andrew did was to put up his brass nameplate on the front door.

Fawn and Minnie filled the cupboards and closets while the moving man arranged the furniture. The children ran from room to room peeking into every closet and opening every door again and again.

In a corner of the property back of the house the children discovered something they hadn't seen before—the riding stables. Doves cooing from under the eaves failed to soften their disappointment at the first sight of the stalls. They were empty.

Sistie was the first to give tongue to it. "If we're going to be so rich," she said with a toss of her curls, "then why can't we have horses to ride? My goodness, we could go for hours back into those canyons up there." She pointed to the rolling hills.

Her father stopped and held up his hand. "Children, there's something we'd better settle right now. In the first place, I want to make it quite clear that we are not now— nor ever will be—rich. Second, we do not own one inch of this home. We are only living here temporarily through the kindness of the church. No pastor could ever afford a home like this," he smiled. "Just make the most of the few years we can live here. We may not always be so fortunate."

He looked at each of his offspring in turn. "Do you

understand?" All bobbed their heads. "However, I do agree," he added, "that it would be fun to have some animals around. Therefore you children may raise rabbits." There was a joyous outburst. "Perhaps you can even earn some money by selling them to your classmates."

Once Andrew had reached a decision, he lost no time in translating it into action. When the children arrived home from school a few days later, they found four empty rabbit hutches lined up next to the stables. (Bud had announced loftily that rabbits were for "kids" and he had better things to do with his time.)

Early Saturday morning all the family piled into the Ford and went to price rabbits. Sistie, Lolly, Duck, and Pidge were allowed to pick out one doe apiece. Andrew then bought a big fat buck which he said was for everybody. The children found their Papa's reasoning a little strange, but they were so elated at each having a rabbit of his very own that it never even occurred to them to raise the question.

A few weeks later at the dinner table Andrew announced that the rabbits were soon to become parents. Thereafter, the children dashed out the first thing every day to see if the new babies had arrived. Several days passed. The does had made nests and Andrew was sure the babies had been born. But he impressed on the children that they were not to disturb the rabbits by peeking.

Then one morning, after the daily inspection of the pens (from two feet away), the children ran back into the house, tears streaming down their faces.

"Mamma! Papa! They're all dead!" the children shrieked hysterically. Everyone rushed back to the pens. Sure enough, some marauding animal had attacked and killed all the baby rabbits.

The children could not be consoled in their grief. But

the time came for them to leave for school. Fawn and Andrew sat in the kitchen relaxing over a cup of coffee.

"I feel so sorry for them." Fawn looked at her husband over her cup with wide, guileless eyes. "It will be quite some time until another litter is born. And then, who knows? The same thing may happen."

Andrew nodded, wondering what was coming.

Then Fawn said, "Why don't we take that puppy the Pierces offered us? The mother has always seemed so sweet. She's such a clean, slick-haired little thing—I'm sure her puppy would be perfect for the children."

Fawn smiled appealingly up at her husband. "It will be good for the children to learn to train the dog while they're all young, don't you think? You could make a warm box for it on the back porch until it's old enough to sleep in the stables."

"I'll promise this much," said Andrew. "I'll think it over."

At six o'clock that evening Andrew tiptoed in the back door and put a small box on the floor. From it he lifted a tiny brown puppy, cradling it gently in his big hands.

"Minnie, come and look. This is a surprise I brought home for the children—to take their minds off of what happened this morning."

Minnie stroked the puppy's forehead with the tip of her finger. "She iss so cute. She iss like a brown bunny rabbit herself."

Andrew slipped the ball of fur into his coat pocket and walked into the front room. Fawn was coming down the stairway with one little boy, freshly washed and combed, on either side of her.

Andrew stood at the foot of the stairs and patted his pocket. "Can you guess the surprise Papa has for you, children?" he asked.

"A puppy dog!" Duck shouted.

Andrew looked quizzically at Fawn and raised his eyebrows. "How on earth did he guess?"

Pidge wrinkled up his nose. "Because, while Mamma was washing our hands, she asked us if we had a puppy dog, what would we name it," he replied. "Where's the puppy, Papa? Where is it, quick! I want to see it." He pulled on Papa's coattail.

Andrew put a hand in his pocket and put the puppy on the floor.

"She's so nice and brown—*Brownie*—" Pidge said. Then he whooped, "Let's call her Brownie!"

Duck held Brownie up to his face and whispered in her ear, "Do you like your name, little girl dog, huh?"

Brownie looked up and yawned sleepily.

"She tried to say yes," Pidge exclaimed. "She likes her name. Now let me hold her and whisper in her ear."

The neighborhood, to say the least, was conservative. The broad, quiet streets were lined with palms or pepper trees. The houses on either side of these avenues were for the most part low, rambling structures of California redwood, set back in sloping, closely clipped lawns and geometric hedges kept neat and immaculate by the ministrations of Japanese gardeners.

Here lived, for the most part, families of the entrenched well-to-do: bankers, lawyers, the prosperous merchants, descendants of Spanish land-grant families, or those who had come out from the east with their fortunes, like their reputations, already made. The *nouveau riche*, the upstarts, had not yet penetrated here.

From the outset it was evident that the neighborhood intended to take no notice of the advent of the pastor and his obstreperous family. No cards were left, no phone calls exchanged. No one ever appeared at the back door to borrow a cup of sugar.

Now and then, a lace curtain might be discreetly twitched as the old Ford chugged up the street. Eyes might be raised from behind a private hedge in a momentary manifestation of curiosity, but that was all. However, if the neighbors had it in mind to continue their indifference they were reckoning without the personality of the preacher.

He had going for him the perfectly human urge to find out the unknown. Andrew was reasonably certain that no one in the neighborhood had ever had a peek into the exotic garden, let alone the inside of the remarkable house. He also felt intuitively that they were longing to do so.

For bait, there were Fawn's gifts as a hostess, and Minnie's genius as a baker of Swedish pastries. Family by family, up and down the street, the invitations went out. Before long the telephone was ringing and visitors' footsteps were clattering up the walk. They had the preconceived notion that preachers were as poor as the proverbial church mice and they were curious about these people. Fawn was glad they were so taken with the house they hardly looked at the preacher's ordinary furnishings. Fawn had a flair for making spillovers from the missionary box not only into pretty clothing, but upholstering pillows or accessories. Guests were treated so royally they forgot to criticize.

It was a crowning triumph for Andrew when it became clear that the neighborhood children would much rather play in the pastor's backyard than in the park across the street. Soon they were begging to be allowed to go along to Sunday school with their new friends. In no time the family Ford rumbled off, weighted down to the mudguards with neighborhood youngsters of assorted ages and sizes.

For a while Andrew was so pleased with the success of his strategem that he accepted the inconvenience of the old car without a qualm. But eventually he began to make increasingly derogatory remarks about the vehicle and to wax eloquent about the dangers of overloading. The family got the idea that Papa was about to spring a surprise, although they did not quite know what it would be.

Then came the day when Andrew showed up, not with the old car, but with the monstrosity described in the opening chapter as the Hallelujah Chariot. He was so proud of the new car that he couldn't wait to take everybody—Clyde, Paul, and Phillip included—on a picnic into the hills up past Pasadena.

The Hallelujah Chariot was stacked high with food and people. Andrew whistled as he drove the shiny vehicle toward the mountains. The car, under its load of eleven passengers, chugged faithfully up Fair Oaks Avenue into the foothills below Mount Lowe. The mountain road wound up and up, crossing several small streams. Andrew nonchalantly plowed through them all, shooting up sprays on either side.

At last he nosed the Chariot under a big sycamore tree and everybody got out. For a time, the children and their uncles picked wild holly and waded in the brooks. After lunch the women stacked the empty food baskets on the floor of the car. Andrew, finding a comfortable position for his long legs, settled himself in the back seat for a nap. The children cajoled Mamma and Nana into taking a hike. Paul and Phillip hoisted the two small boys piggyback and they all started up a winding path.

An hour or so later, they were making their way back, when they heard someone yell. Everyone stood still, looked at one another, and listened. "*Help!*" Now they could hear it clearly.

Fawn's eyes grew as big as saucers. "It's *Andrew!*" she cried. She lifted her skirt and broke into a run.

Legs of all sizes rushed ahead of her. When the children rounded the bend in the road, looming above the back seat where they had last seen their Papa were the head and shoulders of a big black bear. Then they saw Papa underneath. The bear was straddling him, licking his face.

The twins picked up pebbles, and threw them, scaring the bear away. Andrew sat up. He looked as though he had seen a ghost.

"Get her started quick," he shouted to Phillip, pointing to the front end of the Chariot. "Crank fast, Boy, the bear might come back. She ate most of the food in the baskets. She's probably going for her cubs now." He shook his finger, "One slap from that she-bear could send anybody into eternity." The thought propelled him to action. "Get the children in the car," he called to Fawn. He vaulted over the seat into the front. While Phillip cranked, Andrew worked the spark lever.

Everyone had barely piled in, when Andrew started the car downhill with a roar. He accelerated full speed and the tires spun so fast they threw gravel. Down, down, down, the Chariot roared over the winding road.

"Andrew, you frighten me more than the bear," Fawn screamed. "You'll kill us all! Slow down!"

Andrew tramped on the brake pedal. Nothing happened. He pushed again and his foot went clear to the floorboard. He worked his foot up and down frantically. Still nothing happened. Then he realized he had burned out the brakes.

"Hang on," he yelled. "She has no brakes! If I can make it to a level spot I'll turn her back up a hill."

The children, unaware of any danger, laughed and shouted with glee as they careened around curves, this way and that, at breakneck speed.

Fawn, clutching Pidge about the waist, prayed aloud. Andrew couldn't pray; he was too busy.

Nana hung on to Duck and yelled at the twins above the roar of the engine, "Get out on each side and drag your feet. That'll slow us down."

Paul and Phillip scrambled out on the running board on either side of the car. They grabbed the leather straps and dropped to the road. Dust filled the air as they dragged their heels in the gravel, but the effort was futile.

Andrew herded the wild car around a curve. The children laughed harder than ever. "You children hush back there," Andrew yelled. "We may not come out of this alive."

At the bottom of the hill was a stream with rocks jutting up from the creek bed. Andrew drove the car straight into it. Cr-r-runch! It hit a large boulder; the back end flipped up. The beautiful brass radiator burst and a geyser of boiling water shot up into the air. The car quivered, then settled back down on its rear tires, and rested there, axle-deep in the stream.

For a moment there was dead silence. Nana got up from the floor, looked out, and saw the twins sitting in the stream. She thought they were crying, but they were laughing so hard tears ran down their cheeks.

In a moment all but Andrew had picked themselves up and had given way to an outburst of relieved giggles.

Still clutching the wheel, Andrew wiped beads of perspiration from his face. He looked dolefully at his precious Chariot, which continued to spout steam.

"And he shall give an Angel charge over thee, to keep thee in all thy ways," he said in a shaky voice. "They shall bear thee up in their arms, lest you dash your foot against a stone."

"Huh," Nana said, "I thought we were all angels there for a minute. Boy, we were really flying."

"I never knew that when it said 'Bear thee up in their arms' they meant a real live bear," Pidge said as an afterthought.

Andrew patted the car ruefully. "Thank Heaven it's only the radiator. Nothing that can't be fixed."

Fawn didn't seem to share his jubilation. She would not have grieved had the damage been irreparable.

To Fawn, who wanted all things to be gracious and beautiful, the Chariot was another cross to bear. This, perhaps, was the heaviest one of all. It had been an article of faith with her that she could influence people for the better through beauty, as Andrew thought he could through education. Bravely, but with the utmost discretion, she always managed to wear the most becoming, modish clothes and to set her table with the loveliest crystal, china, and silverware that she could lay hands on. It was her conviction that the Lord had put beauty into the world to bring joy.

Now she was to be afflicted henceforth by being forced to appear in public in the company of this ugly, malformed, misbegotten instrument of transportation. But, as in the case of the unusual people that her husband sometimes brought home, she knew it was required of her role in life that she accept it. She did so—without complaint.

For the children, however, it was a different matter. The Hallelujah Chariot put in its appearance on the night they first learned of the miracle in Papa's early life. From that time on, it was bound up inextricably with their memories of their father and they loved every inch of that grotesque, unbeautiful big car.

13

A New Member of the Family Arrives

Soon after the family was settled in the big Japanese mansion, Nana came over to spend the day. Nana was impressed with the house; she was much more moved by the load of work that had fallen on her daughter's shoulders.

Almost imperceptibly, the duties of pastoring the large mother church increased the demands on Andrew's energies and his time. Not only did he have a larger flock to call on, but a far greater volume of church business deluged his office. He was also still studying mornings at the University for his Bachelor of Divinity degree. Therefore much of the increased burden fell on his wife. Furthermore, the parishioners seemed to regard the manse as "open to the public" which meant a further drain on her energies.

The day after Nana came to call, she telephoned Andrew at the church office. "Andrew, I hardly slept a wink last night," she said. "I'm worried about Fawn. She simply cannot keep up the pace. In my opinion, she's headed for a nervous breakdown."

Andrew's voice shook. "What . . . how . . . did she say anything to you to indicate this was the case?"

"No, of course not," replied Nana indignantly. "You know she would never do a thing like that. Fawn is the sort who'll go right on until she collapses, then apologize for it. But I did notice one thing I had completely forgotten, something she used to do as a child. When she was upset, she used to walk around the house clenching and unclenching her hands. Yesterday I saw her do that and I was frightened. I knew she was making those fists to keep herself under control. I don't even think she's aware that she is doing it."

Before Andrew could say anything, Nana announced that she was moving in to take charge. Her son-in-law accepted gratefully and went to get her in the Chariot.

Just as they reached home, a messenger came up the walk with a telegram.

"I don't know why, but these things always scare me," he said as he scanned the yellow slip of paper. "Oh, no," he groaned. "Here, read this." He extended the telegram to Katherine. "Am I ever glad you're here. I'm going to need some good strong moral support."

Nana's eyes moved along the page forming the words on her lips. " 'Will arrive Thursday on the four-forty, signed Matthew Brand.' " She looked up at Andrew. "Who's Matthew Brand? Another Texas evangelist?"

"No!" came the quick exclamation. "I'm sure you remember our writing you from Portland about the wealthy man and his blind wife who were so kind to us during our pastorate in the little church on Burnside Street? Matthew was one of those, you know, who gave so generously to the building fund. We can never repay that kind man," he went on. "But we do owe him a little interest. Come." He picked up Nana's luggage. "You must help me break the news to Fawn. As usual, I've put my foot in it again."

Nana's short legs forced her to take two steps to his one. "But how can I help, Andrew, if I don't know what you've done?" She pulled on his coattails.

"I've been corresponding with Matthew for some time now," Andrew answered. "I found out he was in a little trouble. I told him that if he ever needed a friend, our home was his for as long as he lived. Only I—I didn't dream it would be this soon. I planned to tell Fawn when the time came. I—I—" He looked helplessly at Nana. "What shall I do?"

Nana cocked her head. "I can hear Fawn playing her guitar in the den," she whispered. "She must be giving a lesson. Tell me, if that man is so wealthy, why does he need to come here to live?"

"Tell you later," Andrew said. He tapped on the den door. "Someone is here to see you," he called softly. "When you're finished, you'll find us in the kitchen."

"We're just finishing now," Fawn replied. "I'll be right there."

A few minutes later she came trotting into the kitchen. "Mother!" she exclaimed, throwing her arms around Nana. "What's going on around here? You rascals are up to something!"

"We have a couple of surprises for you," her husband said, trying to sound casual. "Number one—Katherine is moving in for a while to help out. Isn't that wonderful?"

Fawn threw her arms around her mother again and cried, "Oh, Mother, Mother, how I need you! You'll love this beautiful home." She patted Nana affectionately. "But you aren't to work here, darling."

"Not to work!" gasped Nana. "But that's what I came for."

"No! You're our guest. The children will be tickled pink. I can't wait to see their faces when they find out."

Fawn looked from one to the other in perplexity. "You two don't seem to be very happy. What on earth is the matter?"

Andrew unfolded the telegram. "Read this," he said. "You know your mother's uncanny way of smelling out things to come. It looks as though she's arrived just in time."

Fawn read the telegram and looked up inquiringly. "Matthew Brand arriving for a visit? Drew, how wonderful! I can't imagine why you're acting this way. Mother and he will have a wonderful time together. Oh, Mother," she went on, "he is the most elegant, courtly, handsome man you ever met." She jumped up and looked at the telegram again. "Four-forty tomorrow," she gasped. "Andrew, mercy, we'll have to hurry and move our clothes. . . ."

Andrew looked at Katherine pathetically. "You tell her, Katherine," he sighed. "I haven't the heart."

Nana forced a smile. "This elegant, courtly, handsome man isn't coming for a visit, Fawn. He's moving in for keeps."

"What tact!" Andrew moaned, holding his head. "I could have said that myself."

Fawn blinked her eyes rapidly, as though trying to absorb the dimensions of the change that was about to take place.

"I'm glad he's coming," Nana said. "There's nothing like an elegant, courtly, handsome man to perk up a tired, middle-aged woman. I'll move in with Lolly."

"Drew," Fawn said suddenly, "is Matthew Brand b-r-o-k-e?"

"Dead broke," Andrew said sadly. "When Sarah died, he got rid of his business. Through the years, since we left Portland, he's been swindled out of everything he owned. For months, now, he's been paying his hotel bills by selling off his antiques. You can see why I asked him to live with us," Andrew pleaded. "I knew you admired him. Somehow I can't think of that man as a burden to anyone. But I did mean to tell you before he appeared." He leaned over and

kissed Fawn on the cheek. "This telegram is a surprise to
me, too."

"Oh, that poor, poor darling man," Fawn sighed with
a rush of sympathy. "We must make him feel loved and
wanted. He can be a grandfather to the children. They'll
adore that." Then, giving Katherine a quick, guilty look,
she rushed on, changing the subject. "We'll have to hurry
and dust the spare room and cut flowers for his bedside
table. Andrew, remember how he always had flowers everywhere?"

"How old did you say he is, Andrew?" Nana asked,
absently.

"I didn't," Andrew said, and then added hastily as
Nana's mouth opened, "but he's about seventy-six, I think.
A very *young* seventy-six, to be sure."

"Saints above," Nana moaned. "He's old enough to be
my father. You know what they say about old fools," she
laughed. "I think I'll go to Lolly's room and look over my
wardrobe. He may be an old fool with young ideas."

The next afternoon, Nana modishly dressed in a pale
blue suit, arranged the flowers on the bedside table in the
spare room while Fawn brought in her best brocade chair
and placed it beside the window.

"This will make a good place for Matthew to relax,
away from the hubbub of the children." She looked out the
window toward the fig trees.

"Since he's been living in hotels for so many years,"
Nana replied, "he needs a pool of quiet he can call his own.
This place usually resembles the lobby of the Waldorf and
Grand Central Station all rolled into one. After all, Andrew
thinks his parish starts at the front door, goes around the
entire world, and ends at the back door." A case in point
was the prospective arrival of Matthew Brand.

The children were excited at his coming to live in the

manse. They had never known a grandfather and were eager to make believe he was their very own. This day they didn't have to be prompted to wash and comb for a change; they were scrubbed and impatiently waiting for Papa when he cranked the Chariot.

Matthew Brand was a man still handsome, who carried himself erect. His cheeks were pink; his hair silver-white. A neatly trimmed goatee added just the right touch of dignity to his appearance. He was immaculately dressed in a black jacket, winged white starched collar, black tie, dark gray trousers, black derby, and soft leather boots. His gold-headed walking stick finished the picture of quiet elegance.

"He looks like a skinny Santa Claus!" Duck exclaimed.

"He does not," Sistie corrected him. "He looks like a doctor. He has a goatee like Doctor Paul."

"How would you and Duck like to show Brother Brand the Chariot?" their father asked. "Bud and I will bring the luggage."

Duck reached for Matthew's hand. "Are you Papa's brother?"

"We are brothers in Christ," he said gently, as he took each boy by the hand. "Where is this Chariot your Papa was talking about?"

"It cost three hundred dollars and our old Ford," Pidge volunteered.

The children's companion leaned back and laughed. "Well, now, do you suppose Elijah went to heaven in anything this fancy?" He pointed at the car with his walking stick.

"Nope," Duck answered. "Mamma doesn't think it looks like a Chariot. Mamma doesn't think it's fancy at all—and if Mamma doesn't, I guess God doesn't either."

Katherine, Fawn, and Minnie were waiting expectantly

when the big car rolled into the driveway. Fawn threw the door open wide. The women of the household hurried to greet their guest.

Matthew bowed over Fawn's hand and raised it to his lips. "The past years have made you more beautiful than ever, if that is possible," he said gallantly. "Is this your sister?" he inquired, looking at Katherine.

"I'm Fawn's mother. If you keep up this flattery," she said, "you and I are going to get along famously. I can see that right now."

Minnie extended her hand bashfully. "Do you remember dat Swedish girl in Portland who used to make your wife laugh with her accent?"

Brother Brand took both of Minnie's hands in his. "Minnie Olson!" he exclaimed. "Sarah was always so enchanted at the way you testified in church. She would be pleased to know that you are here with Fawn and Andrew."

Bud and his father carried Brother Brand's two large trunks in the back door and set them on the kitchen floor. Andrew walked to the front entry and spoke to his friend.

"I think it would be easier to unpack the trunks in the kitchen and carry your belongings upstairs," he said. "We can store the empty trunks in the loft of the stables."

"Come with me, everybody," Matthew said, taking Fawn's hand. "Let's go open the trunks."

They surrounded Matthew as he unlocked the first one. He lifted the lid and took out a box wrapped in flannel.

"I had to sell most of my things," he said with a wistful sigh, "but I was determined not to come to you empty-handed." He placed the box in Fawn's hands. "This was Sarah's. She designated it for you, many years ago."

Fawn opened the box. "Sterling silver!" she exclaimed. "A dozen of everything! Oh, Matthew, how exquisite. I never dreamed I would ever own sterling." She leaned over and kissed him.

"There are more than the place settings." He lifted out a silver gravy boat. "I'm sure there are several vegetable dishes and platters somewhere." He peered into the cavernous depths. "Sarah and I both decided long ago that beautiful servers like these belong on the Lord's table in a manse."

"What a lovely thought!" Fawn said, smiling at him. "And I agree with you heartily. Andrew knows that. Too many people think the Lord wants everything unadorned."

"Andrew," Brother Brand said, pointing to a box in the trunk, "will you indulge an old man and take out the gift that I brought the children? I picked it up in Germany the last time I was there."

Andrew lifted another box that was almost three feet long and set it on the table with a grunt. The children jostled each other in their efforts to see what it contained.

There sat a pearl and gold inlaid music box. Matthew opened the lid, reached under a glass, and gently pulled a lever. A German lullaby, sounding as though it was played on a harpsichord, tumbled forth.

"There are eight numbers on the roll," Matthew pointed out to his awe-struck young audience. "If you're careful, the music box should last as long as you live and longer. It's now over a hundred years old."

Brother Brand played several selections, then reached into the trunk and picked out another box, a small, square one. He opened it and held up a gold watch encrusted with gems. His eyes were bright as he handed it to Andrew, who held it fondly for a moment, then pressed the stem that opened the face.

"I remember this beautiful watch," he said. "It was Sarah's. This is the watch that chimes the hour." He held it out for the children to admire. "I remember Sarah listening for the time when she wore it pinned to her dress. My! What an honor!"

"There are diamond and pearl cuff links to match."
Brother Brand handed Andrew another box. "Sarah bought
those for me when I purchased the watch. I want you to
have these, too."

"Mercy, mercy," Andrew chuckled. "Where would a
preacher ever wear beauties such as these?"

"At the University functions," Fawn replied quickly.
"They'll dress up that old black suit of yours, if anything
will."

Matthew looked at Katherine and Minnie with a twinkle
in his eyes. Then he lifted up a small box and took out two
rings.

"These were my wife's dinner rings," he said, handing
one to each of them. "After Sarah lost her sight, she was
constantly knitting, crocheting, tatting, writing, and reading Braille. These rings should never lie hidden away in a
container. They would lose their sparkle. They belong on
busy fingers."

Minnie put the jade ring on a finger of her right hand.
"Aye better buy rubber gloves."

Nana slipped the diamond onyx ring on her third finger.
She turned her hand to catch the sunlight. "I was born for
jewels like this," she said softly.

"I guess I come by my love of luxury honestly," Fawn
quipped dryly. "Oh, Matthew," she said, hugging the older
man, "we're so happy to have you with us."

With this joyous arrival, a beloved friend became a
new member of the family.

14

To Give and Give and Give Again

A few days later, Dr. Easton, a medical missionary, arrived with his family for an indefinite stay. Accustomed as they were by now to strange visitors, Dr. Easton's very presence filled the members of the pastor's household with awe.

The medical missionary's white linen suit and pith helmet gave him a dramatic look. His emaciated face above his frail, stringy body bespoke sacrifice. His prematurely gray hair gave credence to his tales of long hours of toil in the vineyards of the Lord. However, it was the pockmarks on his skin that, above all, fascinated the younger boys. They couldn't help staring at Dr. Easton, but they tried to do so out of the corners of their eyes, always watching guiltily for a signal from their mamma. Whenever they got her alone they asked what caused the pocks in the man's face. But Fawn wouldn't take the hint. The less said the better.

Chubby, pleasant-faced Mrs. Easton and Hari, the Hindu girl whom the Eastons had adopted, were dressed in identical white saris, which fascinated Sistie and Lolly. The Eastons had with them their twelve-year-old twins, Lloyd and Mark. The boys wore English knickers, Eton caps, and broad white collars. Their outfits made Bud, Duck, and Pidge snicker.

The visiting youths were settled in the room over the stable with the pastor's boys. The missionary family was ensconsed in their rooms. Late that afternoon Bud, Duck, and Pidge gathered in their new quarters to discuss the missionaries.

"All they did the whole afternoon was drink tea, tea, tea," Bud complained. "I'll warrant neither of those boys knows how to play baseball or swim. I can't imagine what we are going to do to have any fun," he fumed.

"Perhaps we might play a spot of soccer or cricket," Mark Easton said, putting his head around the door of Bud's room in the stable. "Or, if you like," he went on in a patronizing tone, "I'll be glad to show you how we hunt elephants in Mysore."

Bud blushed. "That would be great," he said lamely, hoping his younger brothers would keep their mouths shut. He could just imagine Duck or Pidge saying, "What's a spot of cricket?" or "How do you play soccer?"

That evening at dinner, Doctor Easton looked across at Andrew. "What a beautiful family you and Fawn have." He winked. "Years ago, when we were freshmen at the University, did you ever think we would multiply like this? It looks as if you are raising enough missionaries to convert a whole heathen country."

"James, you know I always felt I was called to go to the mission field myself." Andrew gave a wistful smile. "Remember the plans we once made? Every time I think, 'Now I shall be able to go,' something always comes up to prevent it."

"Like us," said Lolly, with a giggle.

Doctor Easton turned to Fawn, noticing how stiffly she was sitting on the edge of her chair. He weighed his answer carefully.

"I have three children, counting Hari whom we have

adopted." He nodded toward the nine-year-old Indian girl sitting next to Lolly. "But it is not easy to take children to the mission fields. You're young." He looked steadily at Andrew. "If I were you, I would wait a few years until the children are older. Besides, they need you here. I see that Pasadena College not only trains teachers, but missionaries as well.

Fawn sat back in her chair. "They've just added a nursing school, also," she said. "My, who would have thought our young denomination would grow by leaps and bounds this way?"

"Not only a nursing school, but one of the finest music departments in the state," Andrew interjected. "It's high time that the churches supported an academic program. One of these days that school will be a university like U.S.C. You mark my words."

All through the dinner hour, Duck kept staring at Doctor Easton. At last he could restrain himself no longer. "What happened to your face," he burst out. "Did an Indian shoot you with a BB gun?"

There was an awkward silence. "Son," Fawn said blushing, "where are your manners?"

Duck dropped his head. "I'm sorry. I only wondered." His lips quivered. "I thought he knew they were there."

Doctor Easton reached across the table and patted Duck's hand. "That's all right, my boy," he said reassuringly. "I know they're there and I understand your curiosity."

"He certainly does," Mrs. Easton said pleasantly. "And he doesn't mind your asking about his face. He loves to talk about India, especially the smallpox epidemic. Many souls were won after James had saved their lives. Those pockmarks have opened many doors."

Everyone at the table sat spellbound for an hour while

the medical missionary described the epidemic and the heroic part the missionaries and the Nazarene hospital had played in saving lives.

Doctor Easton, as guest speaker at the Sunday service, told graphic, heartrending stories of India, in which he eloquently portrayed the plight of the poor. At the close of his talk, he made an appeal for offerings to buy rice which would be sent to his mission station and passed out to the needy. As the members of the congregation filed past the narthex, they were each given a small white box to use for their offering which was to be brought back the following Sunday.

That week, Doctor Easton and Andrew spent long hours talking about India and praying for its people. To help awaken the citizens of Los Angeles from their indifference, they hired a printer to produce leaflets by the thousands showing photographs of starving children with swollen bellies lying naked in the streets.

The children of the two families toured the neighborhood leaving the leaflets on porches or passing them out on the streets. Every night they limped wearily to the appointed corner and waited for their father to come by in the Chariot and pick them up. When Lolly dragged herself to the car, she moaned and groaned much louder than the others. She was hoping Papa wouldn't find out that she had taken her leaflets to the nearest sewer, thrown them in, and played hopscotch on the sidewalk until she saw the Chariot coming.

The next Sunday morning crowds filled the sanctuary and lined the aisles to hear Doctor Easton. His message stirred the hearts of his listeners as he recounted one incident after another that he had personally witnessed in India. Then he asked Hari to stand. He told how, when just a baby, she had been married to a man of eighty, and how, a few years later, when her husband died, she was supposed to be burned with him on the funeral pyre.

"It was providential that I happened along that day,"
Doctor Easton said. "I was able to rescue this child and take
her into our home, where we raised her as our own
daughter." He smiled down at her. "She says she wants to
become a medical missionary," he went on. "I have brought
her to America to go to school so that she will be able to
realize this ambition. I will ask her to give the closing
prayer."

Hari stepped to the center of the platform and placed
her delicate, tiny hands together. "Oh, loving Savior, thank
you for letting me come to this good country. If you will
allow me to become a doctor, I promise not to disappoint
you. Help them to realize that Christians care about their
bodies as well as their souls. Thank you, my wonderful God.
Amen."

Andrew stepped into the pulpit. While the organ
boomed out "Marching to Zion," the ushers guided the
congregation past the large containers that had been placed
on the altar to hold the offerings and also the little white
alabaster mite boxes.

The congregation moved forward. Fawn stood by the
family pew with Katherine and the children. There was a
troubled look on her face. She was quite aware that her
husband, in order properly to entertain the Easton family,
had greatly overspent the budget. She also knew that since
there had been several emergencies among the church's
needy, there was no more money in the family coffer. Yet,
when she looked gratefully at her own healthy, happy
brood, thought of her attractive home, her heart was filled
with compassion for the children of India. She so desperately wanted to give. But what did she have left of value?
She stepped out into the aisle.

Fawn's finger touched her wedding ring. She turned
it around and around. Her feet carried her slowly forward.
At every step she struggled with her emotions, trying to

check her impulse. But the hungry children kept appearing in her mind's eye.

She passed the first basket, keeping her eyes straight ahead. She came to the second basket. She started to move on, then as she passed, she quickly pulled the ring from her finger and dropped it in.

Her gesture was not lost on Katherine, following close behind. Furtively Nana slid from her finger the lovely dinner ring Brother Brand had given her; she dropped it quickly into the basket and with the same gesture caught up her daughter's wedding band. She closed her fingers tightly over it. Expressionless, she marched on. Katherine was angered by the financial circumstances which had moved Fawn to surrender her most cherished possession. She was even angrier with herself because she had not as much charity in her heart as her daughter.

When the pastor found out that his wife had put her wedding ring into the mission offering basket—Katherine saw to it that he did find out—his heart was torn. At one moment he felt like putting on sackcloth and ashes; the next, he rejoiced that her heart was so touched by human need. He sat at his desk with his head in his hands, reproaching himself that it was too late to retrieve the ring. He looked up at the calendar on the wall; it was April 5, 1917. He turned the leaf and circled May 18.

"I'll buy her a ring for her birthday, somehow," he promised himself, looking at the calendar. He had six weeks in which to save the money.

Early the next morning the household was awakened by shouting in the street. Andrew ran to the window. A man, sitting on the hood of a truck, was yelling at the top of his lungs.

"EXTRA! EXTRA! READ ALL ABOUT IT!

UNITED STATES DECLARES WAR ON GERMANY!"

The young minister hurried to the street and bought a paper. The bold black headlines jumped out at him from the page. It was April 6, 1917. The United States had joined Great Britain and France in the "war to make the world safe for democracy." Shakily, he walked back into the manse and handed Doctor Easton the paper without a word.

In the next few days, excitement prevailed. It was out of the question now for the Eastons to return to the field. Andrew helped find a furnished house for the family. Arrangements had to be made for the missionaries in India, Armenia, and other countries to come back to America immediately. A thousand added responsibilities fell on his shoulders. Andrew forgot all about his wife's wedding ring.

Overnight, Los Angeles flamed with patriotic fervor. Church basements were turned into headquarters for the Red Cross where missionary societies met to roll bandages from old sheets. Katherine joined the Red Cross Nursing Corps. Andrew was on call with the Chariot so many hours of the day and night that his family rarely saw him.

The real blow fell, though, when he told the children he and Mamma had thought it over, and decided that he should enlist in the Army as a chaplain. The announcement brought shocked silence to the dinner table as five pairs of eyes stared. Then five heads dropped and the tears started to flow. Pandemonium reigned.

Andrew collected his wits, and bellowed above the din. "Wait a minute, wait a minute! I haven't gone yet. I don't even know if they'll take me."

Things calmed down a little then, but dinner that evening was a very subdued affair.

The next day the children could hardly pay attention in school: this was the day of Papa's Army induction. When the bell rang, the three older children pedaled home furiously. Duck and Pidge were sitting on the porch steps awaiting Papa's return.

The Chariot lurched into view at last; Andrew jerked down the ignition lever and left the car snorting in the driveway. He ran to the porch, gathered his children into his arms, and kissed each one just as their mamma came to the door, a picture of anxiety. The look on Papa's face was all the family needed.

Fawn found her voice. "They wouldn't take you!" she exclaimed, clasping her hands.

"No sirree. They wouldn't even consider taking me. But I passed my physical with flying colors," he added hastily.

"Well, then why wouldn't they take you?" Bud interrupted.

"Because of you," their Papa said, "and you and you and you and you," he said, pointing to each child.

Pidge pushed his little finger into his father's closed hand. "Now, aren't you glad you had me?" he demanded with a patronizing air.

April vanished into May. One afternoon Katherine arrived hurriedly at the manse only to disappear into the kitchen. At various intervals, mouth-watering aromas drifted through the swinging doors. The children were ordered outside by Nana to play until suppertime. Fawn was at a meeting and Andrew was at the hospital.

That evening, Fawn was in her place and the children already seated, when Andrew came bounding down the stairway. He went to the kitchen door, put his head in, then glanced at his watch.

"I'm in a hurry, Katherine," he called out. "Come sit down. I have to get back to the hospital. One of my parishioners is terribly ill."

As he spoke, his eye was caught by a huge birthday cake sitting on the sideboard. It was frosted in Fawn's favorite color: pink. Circling it were thirty-three white birthday candles. "Fawn's birthday!" he gasped. "Merciful heavens. I completely forgot."

Katherine put a finger to her lips. "So has she," she smiled. "Go sit down. I have a present for her—YOU can beg forgiveness later."

Sick at heart, Andrew slowly took his place. All eyes turned toward him as they waited for him to say grace. He folded his long hands and began a blessing.

A moment later, he stopped, opened his eyes, and looked across the table at Fawn. Closing his eyes again he prayed with particular fervor, "Oh, God, wilt thou convey to my beloved helpmate my anguish for my unforgiveable negligence to her on this, her birthdate?" Andrew opened one eye a second. "Amen," he ended precipitately.

Fawn looked up and caught her breath. She, too, had forgotten that this was her birthday.

Minnie pushed the swinging door open with her elbow, bringing in a platter of fried chicken which she set down in front of the head of the household. Slyly she pointed to one piece and whispered in Andrew's ear, "See dis piece here? Serve dis to your wife first. Act natural. Ve don't want her to guess."

Andrew looked at the piece of chicken for a moment, then glanced down the table toward Katherine whose face was a mask. A toothpick had been stuck in the chicken's tail. Around the toothpick was Fawn's wedding ring.

Fawn's plate passed down the table. Each one held it for a minute and then handed it along with a poke or a giggle. When it came to Fawn, she kept turning the plate around, wondering what the mystery was all about. Then she saw her wedding ring.

"Andrew!" she burst out, "you darling rascal! You didn't really forget my birthday." She tugged happily at the toothpick. "To think you kept it from me all this time that you got my ring back!"

Her husband had turned beet red. "I'm afraid I don't deserve the credit. Didn't you get the message when I said the blessing, Sweetheart? I'm afraid I was miserably sincere," he sighed. "I intended to buy you a new one. You might know I'd forget. It was your mother who redeemed your ring."

Fawn ran around the table and threw her arms around Nana. "Mother, Mother! You adorable angel," she cried. "Without my wedding ring, my finger has felt so naked." Nana patted her daughter's hand. "Well, when I remembered the inscription, it got me right here." She touched her heart dramatically. "I figured, 'A.O.H. to F.E.G. Forever and Eternity' meant just that."

15

The Northern Relatives' Express Arrives

Opening his stack of mail one morning, Andrew noticed a Canadian postmark. It was a letter from Nels. Hastily he ran his letter opener along the flap. A smile played around his lips as his eyes moved along the typewritten page.

"Dear Drew," he read. "At long last, Mother has been won over to the idea that she must sell the farm. Since it's summer and school is out, I'm planning to take my family down to Minnesota and help her dispose of her property. I hope to convince her that sunny California would be a better place for her to live. Now that Jo and Astrid have both been so tragically widowed by the war, the three women will be much better off away from their memories. Since both girls have university degrees, I am sure they will be able to get good jobs in Los Angeles.

"John is not only farming in North Dakota, he has entered politics. I'm sure he is making a fine judge. I wish Father could have lived to see his children prosper; he always got so much out of life. Since you've always been Mother's favorite, please write her a letter immediately and try to convince her to go to California. I know she will have to listen to you preach a sermon before she can believe you're the pastor of one of the largest churches in Los Angeles. I do hope you have improved since your haystack preaching days. I doubt if I could sit through any more of your boyhood histrionics!"

Andrew glanced out the window for a moment, reflecting. There was an amused look on his face as he read on:

"Besides my wheat farms, I have purchased the Cadillac agency here for Alberta. I can now buy a limousine at wholesale. Being married to a parsimonious Swede, this pleased my wife very much. Then, too, we do need a large car, what with our six children. If I can persuade Mother and the girls to join us, there will be eleven of us driving from Minnesota to Los Angeles.

"When we get Mother and the girls settled, I hope your family will be able to join mine in doing a little sightseeing. You have bragged about Southern California for so long, I feel it is time to investigate it for ourselves—just to find out how *much* you've been exaggerating! I have a very good business manager and we may stay in California for a school year if it is all you say it is.

"Mother is anxious to meet Fawn and the children. Since we planned the trip, our youngsters have talked of nothing else but their cousins in the States. If all goes well, we will be in Los Angeles in about two weeks. Until then, much love. Your big brother, Nels."

That evening after worship, Andrew read the letter to the family. The children jumped from their chairs and whooped and hollered with excitement. Ever since they had heard the full details of Papa's life story, they had been anxious to meet their Swedish relatives.

"What are we going to do about the black bread we've been eating since the war started?" Fawn's forehead wrinkled. "Your mother is accustomed to that wonderful Swedish bread and pastries like we used to have. She'll think our food is pretty stingy. Poor Minnie, her reputation will be ruined."

"Now, Fawn, Mother lives in the United States too, you know," her husband replied. "She knows about the food rationing. But if it will make you feel any better," he said soothingly, "I'll explain to her."

The second week passed and no one arrived. The children took turns walking impatiently in front of the house, looking up the street. They watched each automobile approach hoping one would hold their relatives. One day when Duck was riding his bicycle in the driveway, a long black limousine drove slowly up and parked in front of the manse. When the car stopped, Duck jumped from his bike and ran around the house.

"Mamma, Papa! They're here! They're here!" He dashed in the back door forgetting to stop and put on his slippers. "Our cousins are here. They came in a hearse! Hurry, Papa! Come see!"

Uncle Nels jumped out of the car and opened the door, spilling six eager children onto the sidewalk. The pastor's family poured from the front door. Papa ran down the front walk, hugged his brother, and leaned inside the car.

"Mother, Mother!" He took his mother's thin hand and helped her out of the car.

The children stood by, quietly watching Papa put his arms around his mother in a fond embrace. Mother and son clung to each other and wept. Andrew wiped his eyes. Pulling Fawn forward, he drew her up to Kristina.

"This is my Fawn," he said, looking intently at his mother. Kristina extended her hand. Her black eyes warmed as she appraised her daughter-in-law from head to toe. She turned to Andrew and nodded slightly.

"She is so pretty and frail," she said in Swedish. "Are you sure she is strong?"

Andrew put his arm around his mother and looked at

Fawn lovingly. "Not only strong, Mor," he replied, "but the most wonderful person in the world. Wait until you become acquainted, you'll love her as I do." Kristina inclined her head, agreeing soberly as she watched her son's wife put her arms around Jo, Astrid, and Aunt Anna, trying to make them feel at home.

Belatedly, Andrew began introducing them to Fawn.

"We don't need your help," Jo said, playfully poking Andrew in the ribs. "We've already introduced ourselves. Now let's find out who's who around here with the children. I understand they have some pretty unusual nicknames."

Andrew beckoned to the youngsters. "Line up here in a row, children," he said. "Nels, line your youngsters opposite ours and start first. We'll do this on a mass scale."

Uncle Nels lined up his six according to size. He touched each one on the head as he called out their names: Ethel, Byron, Evelyn, Norman, Wesley, and Baby Ruthie. Papa did the same thing and when he came to Duck and Pidge, Kristina's dark eyebrows arched. She gave Andrew an inquiring look.

"Why don't you call your children by their proper names? Why do you call them after birds?"

"Only the two youngest boys are nicknamed for birds, Mor," he explained. "Sistie nicknamed Bud and Lolly."

Uncle Nels tapped Andrew on the shoulder and indicated the manse. "By your letters," he said, "I knew you were living in some kind of heathen splendor, but I didn't realize it was as grand as this. However, I think we'd better go inside before all of the neighbors fall out their windows and break their necks."

"Heathen splendor, indeed," Andrew snorted indignantly. "Remember, Nels, we don't own this house—the church owns it. On my salary, Brother, we would be the poor preacher's brood. But don't think we are not grateful for God's blessings; through these doors we have been able to reach many unchurched, praise be!"

Fawn glanced uncomfortably from her husband toward the neighbors. "Yes, let's do go into the house." She shooed her brood up the walk. She leaned over to Andrew and whispered, "Don't forget to tell your mother about the bread."

The next morning Uncle Nels and Andrew walked out to the stables to wake eleven sleepy-eyed children. The moans and groans that followed the announcement of breakfast made it evident that the children had been up talking till all hours.

When the two men came back into the kitchen, they found Kristina and Minnie sitting by the stove, dunking black bread in coffee and conversing in Swedish.

"I stay here and eat," Kristina said with finality. She nodded to the dining room door. "No goot for me."

During breakfast Nels apologized to Fawn. "I think Mor is afraid that crystal chandelier will fall on her head." He pointed up to the prisms sparkling in the morning sunlight. "You know, she's never seen a house like this before. It'll take her a while to get used to it."

"I'm more convinced Mother has found a lonesome Swedish girl who makes delicious black bread. She and Minnie are getting along famously. They're even exchanging receipts," Andrew replied, using the old-fashioned word for recipes.

Nels leaned over to his brother and whispered, "Mother will probably bawl you out for not marrying Minnie instead of Fawn."

From then on, every time Andrew or Nels tried to get their mother out of the kitchen to enjoy an outing, or visit a place of interest, she would stiffen up firmly in her chair by the stove and glare at them.

"No goot," she continually repeated. "I stay."

One day Pidge took his cousin Wesley out to the garage to show him the skate coaster he and Duck had made. They could hear Uncle Nels laughing.

"Andrew, this automobile is the funniest thing I have ever seen," he bellowed. "But practical, I can see that. Why don't you get the builder to patent this thing?" he inquired. "You might make a fortune selling the idea to the Ford Motor Company."

"She's quite a conversation piece, too." Papa gave the Chariot a thump. "Our neighbor's little boy named it the Hallelujah Chariot. You'd be surprised how the name has caught on. When I drive around town, I often hear someone say, 'Well, hallelujah, here comes the preacher in his Chariot.' "

The boys hustled around the corner to where the Chariot was parked. "They made fun of our car," Pidge said. "I like it—even if it isn't as nice as yours."

Wesley walked around the back of the automobile and looked up at it. "I like it, too," he volunteered. "Wish Papa would get Uncle Andrew to trade it for our car."

Pidge's eyes got big. "You mean it? Honest?"

"Yep," Wesley nodded. "Every time we ride in our old car Mamma says, 'Don't touch the curtains. Don't get your dirty feet on the cushions,' " he mimicked. " 'Don't, don't, don't!' Whew, all we hear is 'don't.' "

"If Aunt Anna could see the people Papa piles in our car, she would be saying 'don't' all the time." Pidge paused thoughtfully and then glanced up at his cousin. "You know something? Maybe Mamma doesn't like our car very much!"

Southern California held enchantment for the visitors. They found new and exciting places to explore. They discovered new beaches, parks, resorts, and museums.

Andrew and Nels found a home for their mother in a Swedish settlement of Los Angeles. Minnie prepared an old-fashioned smorgasbord as a going-away present to Kristina.

"Ve effen bake white bread," she said to Fawn, as they brought canned fruit up the cellar steps.

After dinner, Fawn suggested Sistie play some of the new tunes written by the young composer, Irving Berlin. The whole family gathered around the piano and sang: "There's a Long, Long Trail a-Winding," "Jeanean, I Dream of Lilac Time," and "It's a Long Way to Tipperary."

Andrew ran upstairs and brought down his harmonicas. He gave one to Nels and said to Sistie, "Play 'Over There.' Come on Nels, let's show them we haven't forgotten how to liven up a party."

The festivities came to an end. Kristina presented Fawn and Minnie with hand-worked dresser scarves. Then she went into her bedroom and brought out a sack of rock candy. With great ceremony she took one piece at a time and pressed it into each child's palm, folding their fingers over the sweet crystal as though it were a gold nugget.

The next Sunday the family and all the relatives filled the pastor's pew. Andrew began his sermon. Suddenly he found himself feeling the way he had when, as a young boy standing on a haystack, he had preached to his mother for the first time instead of the old cud-chewing cows.

As he spoke, he looked out into the congregation, searching his mother's face for a sign of approval. But during his entire dissertation her austere expression never softened. Andrew could come to only one conclusion: in her eyes he was a failure. He came to the close at last, glanced in his mother's direction and noticed that she was nodding. He smiled to himself and ended his sermon with an oratorical flourish.

Afterward he said to Nels, "I was certain that during

the first part of my sermon, Mother was unimpressed. But at the end she nodded in agreement. It was a great triumph to me."

"Don't get so swellheaded, Drew," Nels laughed. "The first part was way over her head. Remember, she's used to hearing Pastor Stigge preach in Swedish. She was probably nodding because she was falling asleep. After all," he concluded with a wicked smile, "a prophet hath no honor in his own home."

16

Two Different Visitors

One morning Fawn telephoned her mother at seven. "I called so early," she explained, "because I wanted to catch you before you left for the hospital. Remember, Friday morning Andrew will receive his Bachelor of Divinity degree. Be sure and ask the twins and Clyde's family. They can all come back here for one of Minnie's famous 'Hoover' dinners."

Friday, the family was dressed in their best and waiting for Papa. But Andrew hadn't appeared. He was out on an emergency call, and they were all worried that he wouldn't get back in time.

"You'd think he could take a half day off to get his degree," Nana remarked dryly. "Lord knows he's worked hard enough for it. That bottle-fed parish should understand once in a while that a preacher's a human being, too."

Before Fawn could reply, she heard Andrew come into the driveway. He left the Chariot hiccuping by the back door and raced up the stairs to change his clothes. In three minutes he came down buttoning his coat.

"Everybody out," he yelled. "The commencement exercises start in thirty minutes."

"School, school, study, study," Sistie muttered. She

glanced at Bud. "Do you suppose Papa will ever stop going to school?"

"Huh-uh!" he declared, shaking his head lugubriously. "He's only got three degrees and three *cum laudes*. I heard him talking to Mamma. He's going to start studying for his Ph.D."

"What?" Sistie shrieked.

"Ask him, if you don't believe me."

Sistie was aghast. "Oh, no! How can he stand it?"

To celebrate Andrew's graduation that evening, Minnie prepared a dinner of unbelievable magnificence—rationing considered. Nana, Clyde, and the twins were seated at the table with the family. Everyone was waiting for Matthew to take his place. At the last minute, Matthew remembered he had left Andrew's present on the dresser. He hurried back to get it and then started downstairs. Suddenly he lost his balance and went rolling down the steps head over heels.

Hearing the clatter, they all ran out to see what had happened. While everyone "oohed and ahed," Phillip and Paul started to pick Matthew up but Nana checked them.

"Don't touch him," she warned. "Call Dr. Bresee." She leaned down and took his wrist, then put her ear to his chest. "He's only been knocked out for a moment," she said. "We mustn't move him, though. There might be internal injuries."

Before Dr. Paul arrived the patient stirred and muttered softly, "Katherine." The doctor proceeded to examine the patient. "All I can find is a broken leg," he said. Then, addressing himself to Matthew, "You're lucky—it might have been your neck. We'll have to take you to the hospital and have the bone set. But in a few days at the most you'll be home." He glanced at Nana. "I expect you already have your nurse picked out."

Matthew grimaced with pain, but he shook his head. "I wouldn't think of asking Ka—Mrs. Galbraith to look after me. I shall ask to be moved to the county hospital."

Nana, standing by the door, stared helplessly at her daughter and son-in-law.

"Why did he have to say that?" she whispered. "Now I can't possibly leave him. He should know that neither of us would allow him to go to a place like that."

Doctor Paul stole a glance at Nana, then he winked at his patient.

For the next two weeks, Katherine nursed Matthew. One day she flew down the stairs wild-eyed, dropped into a chair beside Fawn, and let out her breath.

"Whew!" she exploded. "Do you know what that old coot just did?"

Fawn bit a thread of darning cotton from the spool with her front teeth. "What old coot?" she said absent-mindedly.

"Up there," Nana pointed toward the stairway. "He just tried to put his brand on me!"

Fawn dropped her darning. "He what!" she exclaimed. "You mean he asked you to marry him?"

Nana's head bobbed.

"What would he use for money to support you?"

Nana jumped up and paced back and forth. "I don't know." She perched on the edge of a chair, and stared at the rug. When she looked up, her eyes were sad. "I—wish —I knew how to explain to that sweet, courtly gentleman," she said regretfully. "He's one person I couldn't bear to hurt." She sighed heavily.

"Now I suppose he's wondering what happened to me. I left his back exposed. I guess I'll have to pretend I ran out of rubbing alcohol." She jumped to her feet. "Oh, shoot! Why did this have to happen and spoil such a wonderful friendship?" She smiled at her daughter. "If I can't think of a kind way to refuse him that is also convincing, you may have two permanent star boarders on your hands instead of one."

Katherine started wearily up the stairs. Halfway, she stopped suddenly. "Fawn, listen!" she called. "Do you hear all those sirens! What is it? It sounds like the world is coming to an end."

Fawn jumped from her chair, spilling socks all over the floor. "I haven't the least idea," she said. She ran to the front door and swung it open. "Maybe we've been invaded." The phone began ringing insistently.

"Answer the telephone and find out," Nana said dryly. "Maybe it's Von Richtoffen asking if he can come to dinner."

Fawn raced to the telephone. Nana sprinted down the steps behind her. She poked Fawn and demanded, "Come on, what is it?"

"The Armistice has been signed!" Fawn dropped the receiver on the hook. "Peace forever! I can hardly believe it. No more war. Never, never again."

Nana grabbed her daughter and hugged her. They danced dizzily around the room. Nana let go of Fawn and did a jig. She ran up the stairs calling out, "The war is over, Matthew! The war is over. Whoopee! Let's celebrate!"

School having been let out, the children burst into the kitchen screaming wildly. They stood in front of Fawn dancing from one foot to the other. "Please, Mamma! Everybody is going to Long Beach. There's going to be fireworks. Can we go? Please, Mamma, please."

"We certainly should celebrate," Fawn agreed. "When Papa comes home, we'll ask him if he'll drive us out. Now go and sit on the steps and wait for him. I'll tell Minnie."

The children sat fidgeting, watching the cars go by.

And what a sight it was! Cars with tin cans tied from the rear bumper, cars trailing dishpans after them, horns honking and people running out into the streets to dance and sing.

"Old Kaiser Bill went up the hill to take a look at France. But Kaiser Bill came down the hill with bullets in his pants."

About an hour later the children were still prancing up and down on the steps, when suddenly their chatter was stopped by the sight of a woman coming toward them up the sidewalk. She was dressed all in black—wearing a long, black dress that came clear down to her ankles. A heavy veil hanging down from a broad-brimmed black hat concealed her face, and long black gloves reached up to her elbows. Simultaneously, all heads turned as she glided past, floated up the steps, and rang the doorbell. Fawn answered the door.

"Would you kindly tell the Reverend I must see him at once?" the woman said in a husky voice. "It's a matter of the utmost importance." Fawn glanced at her five impatient children lined up on the steps.

"Reverend Hendricks is out on a call right now," she replied. "Could you possibly come back tomorrow? I have promised the children we'd drive them to Long Beach so that they can see the fireworks. They've been so good about asking him for favors this past year. They do deserve a reward," she finished apologetically.

The lady dabbed at her eyes with a black handkerchief. As she did so, her knees seemed to buckle under her and she fell in a faint at Fawn's feet.

Fawn called for Minnie. Together they helped the woman into the den, where they laid her on Andrew's leather couch. Minnie started to reach for her hat to remove it, but the woman hung onto it with both hands.

Half an hour later, when the pastor arrived, Fawn stopped him at the door and told him about the visitor. "Please don't let her stay any longer than you have to," she pleaded. "I promised the children we'd take them to the beach to watch the fireworks. They're not going to be cheated out of their treat this time."

"You don't get rid of someone who's in trouble," said Andrew bristling. Then he bent over Fawn and kissed her. "Strange that someone would bother us on Armistice Day. It seems like something always comes up at the eleventh hour to take the joy out of life. You can tell the children we are still going to the beach—visitor or no."

He walked decisively into the den where the woman was still lying on the sofa. He had no sooner sat down in a chair when she burst into sobs.

"Oh, Reverend," she wailed, "I don't know what to do. My son is due in on the hospital ship at San Pedro tomorrow." She dabbed at her eyes with a handkerchief. "I came down by train from San Francisco to go see him. While I was in the washroom at the depot—" She choked and paused. "I was robbed! Robbed of everything I possess. My suitcase, my clothes, everything. And I'm all alone in the world. I have no one to whom I can turn, since my dear Cogswell died six months ago."

She peered at Andrew through the heavy veil. "And now my boy will have to see my poor disfigured face. I was in a fire," she went on, between sniffs. "That's why I keep this veil over my face. I'm so self-conscious. I can't bear it when people look at me with pity."

"What a shame!" Andrew patted her gloved hand. By now he was pulsating with sympathy. "You just lie there and rest, Madame. I'll take care of everything. You can stay here tonight. I'll drive you to San Pedro in the morning. In the meantime, we'll fix a room for you and send up a tray. I understand how you feel. No one will bother you, and we'll do all we can to help you, believe me. Now don't worry about a thing. You just rest."

Andrew strode to the kitchen and galvanized the household into action. The children who were waiting in the Chariot were summoned and instructed to help move their bedding back into the stables. Minnie was asked to prepare another tray. Fawn hurried upstairs to get the girls' room ready for the lady guest and to brief Nana.

By the time the Hallelujah Chariot backed out of the driveway, it was five o'clock. The oncoming darkness didn't dampen the children's spirits one bit. They began a game which was the current popular craze called "Stamping." Every time they passed a horse they screamed, licked the tip of a finger, pushed it into the palm of the other hand, and pounded it with a fist. One stamp for a black horse, two stamps for a brown horse, and three stamps for a white horse. The bickering as to who had seen what horse first became so loud that Mamma had to keep looking back and shushing them.

The closer the Chariot got to the beach, the noisier grew the children. But their own private din was lost in the general pandemonium that reigned on the highway. Cars clanked along dragging tin cans, kettles, and dishpans. Fawn decided that for once she could let the children become as noisy as they wished. She eased over close to Andrew and shouted, "I guess we can stand this racket for one day. We should be glad to celebrate. After all, this is the last war we're ever going to have."

Pidge, sitting on one of the jump seats, was close enough to Mamma to hear part of her conversation. He leaned over the seat and tapped her on the shoulder.

"If the war is over and there aren't any more starving Armenians, will you ask Papa if I can have a nickel?"

Fawn relayed Pidge's request. Andrew glanced back at his youngest son. "Tonight the treat's on me, Son. The sky is the limit!" He leaned over to Fawn and quietly amended, "At least five dollars worth of sky!"

The next morning, Minnie was up at her usual early hours. Observing the preacher's household protocol, she tapped on the visitor's door first and called out, "Breakfast is ready." There was no answer. Minnie knocked several more times, still no answer. She opened the door. The room was empty. Minnie flew down the stairs to break the news.

Andrew jumped up so precipitately that he knocked over his chair. He raced to his den. It was as though he already knew the answer. With shaking hands, he rolled back the top of the desk. He shoved his hand into one of the pigeon-holes. His fingers touched and then seized a roll of bills. Overcome with relief, he sagged down into his chair, and mopped his forehead with a handkerchief.

Still breathing heavily, he pulled the rubber band from around the roll. Then he started counting out the bills on his desk. He pulled off the top bill and froze. Under the first bill were pieces of newspaper cut to exactly the same size. He lunged out the door waving the paper in the air.

"We've been robbed!" he cried out. "That woman robbed me. She took everything—my whole month's salary! Call the police! Call the police!"

Hearing the commotion, Nana came running down the stairs. Andrew turned, barged back into the den, and telephoned the police himself. After the phone call, he sat gazing at Nana and limply held up the scraps of newspaper.

"Why did that woman have to pick the very day I got paid? What a stroke of bad luck."

Nana cocked her head at her son-in-law. "Never forget to entertain strangers, lest they be angels unawares," she intoned. "Maybe this will teach you a lesson, young man."

At that moment Fawn walked in the door, looked at Nana, and shook her head; Nana gazed at Minnie and shook her head; Minnie peered at the children who had gathered close to the door of the den—they all shook their heads. They knew Papa would never change. He would entertain, feed, clothe, and be a good Samaritan as long as he lived, regardless of the risk.

The police arrived an hour later. Ceremoniously they questioned each member of the family. The youngsters gave a remarkably accurate description of the mysterious woman. Suddenly one of the detectives, Lieutenant Moore, jumped to his feet.

"That description fits the guy we've been looking for since he escaped from prison six days ago!" he exclaimed.

"Guy—she's a man?" everyone yelled at once.

"Sure she's a man," the detective replied without cracking a smile. "Her name—*his* name is Monte Pope. I'm not surprised he fooled you," he went on. "Before he started his one-man crime wave, he was on the stage as a female impersonator."

Fawn glanced at Andrew out of the corner of her eye. "And you felt so sorry for her—him—it," she giggled. Andrew threw up his hands.

The children were sent off to school. Lieutenant Moore settled down with a serious look on his face. He spoke with great concern.

"I didn't want the children to hear this," he said gravely, "but that man is not only a thief, he's a rapist and a murderer." A general startled intake of breath greeted this revelation. "I just telephoned to have an alert sent out for him," Lieutenant Moore continued. "Also, I'll want to put a guard at the manse until he's captured. We can't take any chances."

"The children must not know we're being guarded," Andrew said. "They would brag about it all over the school."

"Okay," the Lieutenant agreed, "I'll put it this way. We'll give you another houseguest. That way the children won't suspect."

Six days later Andrew rushed in the back door and slapped a newspaper down on the table in front of Fawn. He pointed to the headlines—"Murderer Caught in Police Net."

Fawn hastily scanned the paper and shook her head. "To think we harbored a murderer in this house," she said with a shudder. "Thank goodness they caught him. But the children are going to miss being escorted to school by that new 'secretary' of yours. I don't think we fooled them though. I caught them looking at that bulge under his coat. They figured it out."

That night, during worship, Andrew took time to again impress on his offspring part of one of his favorite scriptures. He read the ninety-first Psalm, then repeated his favorite verse: "For he shall give his angels charge over thee, to keep thee in all thy ways."

The month of November turned out to be unusually severe for Southern California. One cold Saturday night, a shabby young man came to the door and asked to see the preacher. Minnie ushered him into the den to wait for Andrew to come home from painting his church study. When he arrived, Andrew invited the visitor to share the family meal. He noticed the boy's feet were wrapped in burlap so he hurried the guest to the table before the children could notice. While he was waiting for the family to gather at the table, he took his customary place and made an attempt at conversation.

"Everything seems much better after a satisfying meal. Don't you agree, Son?" The boy answered his query with a pathetic grin and a duck of his head.

Later in the evening, after the children were in bed, Andrew closeted himself in the den with the boy. An hour afterwards Andrew charged up the stairs and rushed down the hall into their bedroom. A few moments later he emerged, taking inventory of the clothes over his arm. He discovered an item missing and called to his wife from the top of the stairway.

"Fawn, do we have a pair of shoes that will fit this young man? Last night he was sleeping in a mission and someone stole his shoes. And his suitcase," he hollered. "His feet are cold. We can't send him back home with pneumonia."

Fawn waited at the bottom of the stairs for Andrew to stop yelling. Then she leaned over the railing and called up to him, "Andrew, the only shoes in this house that will fit that young man are on your feet. Matthew's would be much too small."

Papa looked down at his feet and chuckled. He was still wearing his old paint-spattered work shoes. He hurried back to his closet, found a pair, a bounded down the stairway into the den.

When the boy had finished putting on the clothes, Andrew stripped the burlap from his feet and handed him a pair of socks. The stranger slipped into Andrew's bumpy-toed shoes, stomped a foot, and grinned. "Just fits," he said.

Andrew looked at him appraisingly for a moment, then opened a drawer in his desk and took out a small Testament. He opened his wallet, counted out some bills, put them in an envelope, and handed it to the boy.

"Son," he said, "there's enough money for your ticket

to Virginia and plenty for food." He smiled at the boy and
gave him the Testament. "Now, I want you to read the
passages I have marked while you're on the train. Somehow, I feel there are things for you to do in this old world.
Don't disappoint me, Boy, but most of all don't disappoint
God and your mother. I'm sure her prayers brought you
here."

He slapped the lad on the back and ushered him outside. "You'll have to run for the streetcar if you're going
to make that eleven-five. You'll just have time to get your
ticket. God bless you, my son," he said, shaking the boy's
hand warmly.

The next morning a most unusual thing occurred for
a Sunday. As a rule, Andrew was the first one in the car,
impatiently tugging the spark lever. This time everyone else
was already in the Chariot waiting for Papa.

Andrew couldn't find his shoes.

Fawn got out of the car and ran upstairs to help look.
One by one all of the family piled out, including Matthew,
and searched every corner and closet for the indispensable
black oxfords.

Suddenly Fawn backed out of her closet on her hands
and knees. She straightened up. "Did you give the only
pair of dress shoes you possess to that young man last
night?" she demanded with tight lips.

Andrew looked at her in surprise. "An-gel," he choked,
"didn't I have another pair?"

"Andrew Hendricks! You know good and well . . .
You're just always . . ." With a straight back she marched
the children down the stairway into the Chariot. They took
their seats rapidly and sat waiting for Papa.

In a moment he appeared with a sheepish grin on his
face. He approached the car with an exaggerated pretense of
unconcern, spun the crank, and bounded into the seat without looking at Fawn.

The family made the trip to church in dead silence. When they stepped out of the car, there was Papa, resplendent in his swallow-tailed suit, but wearing old shoes spattered with white paint.

Laughter spilled over until tears flowed down each gleaming youthful face. Even Mamma's silence dissolved into reluctant laughter. Standing by the curb, she glanced down at her husband's feet.

"Oh, Drew, it's a good thing you have that platform drape," she said ruefully. "Stay close to the edge while you preach," she warned. "Maybe no one will notice."

"Wave your arms, too," Duck added. "That'll keep them from looking at your feet."

Once on the platform, the pastor pushed his feet as far back under his chair as he could. But as he rose to walk to the pulpit, several people in the choir spied his shoes. First it was a smile on one face, but soon all sixty choir members were grinning broadly.

During the sermon, Andrew stayed as close to the drape around the platform as he could. He finally concluded his dissertation with a feeling of relief. The choir master jumped from his chair and led the congregation in a lively hymn, hoping his minister would escape during the singing. Everyone sang with such enthusiasm, however, that Andrew forgot all about his shoes. He looked back at Fawn to join him in their usual march down the aisle to station themselves at the church door.

Fawn was horrified. She stared meaningfully at his feet. Andrew got the message. He waited for the hymn to end, stepped up beside Johnnie Jones, and whispered in his ear.

The congregation was a little surprised to find the choir master and his wife suddenly stationed at the door of the narthex.

The next morning, bright and early, a special delivery

package came for Andrew. Opening the box, he lifted out white tissue paper to find a pair of black English oxfords. A card read, "From your ever-loving choir."

That afternoon the mail brought another package also containing a pair of shoes. Inside one shoe was a note which read, "Every preacher should have an extra pair just in case." Trying the oxfords on, Andrew walked back and forth admiring them. He picked up the other box and opened the lid.

"There you are, Fawn," said Andrew, jubilantly hugging her. "Cast your bread upon the waters and you see what happens. Yesterday I had one pair of good shoes, half worn-out ones at that. Now I have two brand new pairs and much more expensive ones than I could afford to buy, too. Wouldn't you say that is a hundredfold?"

17

The Headquarters of the Devil

In the early nineteen hundreds, Los Angeles real estate developers had gone "Spanish" with fantastic fervor. They plastered the streets, then the suburbs, and finally the valleys of the Los Angeles area, with names and signs, even though they had only the vaguest notion as to their meaning. But it did give the city a kind of unified character.

Then in 1919, the Armistice seemed to open the floodgates of the world and people poured into Southern California. The predominantly Spanish Los Angeles became a Tower of Babel replete with strange rituals, cults, and religions. The Plaza around which the activities of the first Catholic church had once centered now became a popular haven for soapbox orators and the I.W.W.'s (Industrial Workers of the World).

There was a great burst of new buildings. Architecture ran the gamut from Persian rococo to adobe hacienda, from Elizabethan halls to Nantucket cottage, from Norman castle to Japanese teitaku. Some of the world's greatest authors, artists, actors, and musicians came to bask in the California sun.

The debut of the Philharmonic Auditorium was greeted with acclaim by both the city in general and the preacher's family in particular. Andrew had played a leading role in persuading the clergy of the city to back the Philharmonic Society. He was one of the first ministers to purchase season tickets for every member of his family. Each child soon became familiar with some of the leading musicians of the day. Fawn and Andrew never missed Galli-Curci, Schumann-Heink or the symphonies, John Phillip Sousa's band was a family favorite, especially with little Duck. Fritz Kreisler was Bud's particular hero, while Sistie listened with rapt attention to Rachmaninoff through every matinee. Pidge and Lolly were intensely loyal to Caruso, especially after they heard his rendition of "Pagliacci."

But all the entertainment coming to the Los Angeles area was not of the Philharmonic's high caliber. In Hollywood the millennium of easy money was being ushered in. The movie industry began turning out motion pictures which depicted "high life" to the daydreaming millions who attended the nickelodeons.

Billboards screamed with lurid colors depicting the charms of alluringly clad temptresses lying on tigerskin rugs. When Andrew drove past them he tried to avoid staring at them directly. But, as he told Fawn, "a person can almost hear the lovers breathing asthmatic love words." He was sure he was witnessing the end of the pattern of social behavior as he knew it. He was grieved that his children and parishioners would have to live in this new moral atmosphere.

Throughout the nation, pastors preached against the lowered standards of behavior that were sweeping the film industry. They were shocked by the apparent inability of the movies to portray any emotion with good taste.

Andrew was as shocked as any of his fellow churchmen, but at the same time recognized that here existed a latent force for education potentially more powerful than any yet discovered. Time and time again, in conferences with other pastors, he pleaded with them, warning repeatedly that since wickedness was more flamboyant than virtue, the primrose path would be the easier one for the coming generation to follow. Several steps were taken for improvement. The Hayes Office was formed for self-regulation of the industry; the Federal Council of Churches, which had recently come into being, brought organized pressure for better movies.

Yet the attitude of the church remained the same: moving pictures were equated with sin—with a capital "S." Andrew knew that someday the church would realize its mistake, but for the present his hands were tied.

Katherine disagreed completely with the prevailing church attitude toward the motion picture industry. But in order to spare her son-in-law any embarrassment, she usually kept her opinions to herself. Every now and then however, she couldn't resist giving him a little dig about what she called the "Holy Inconsistency" of the church.

One day when she read in the newspaper of a stereopticon slide program to be shown in a local church, she couldn't refrain from calling Andrew at his office.

"Andrew," she cooed, "will you please explain to poor, stupid me the difference between a motion picture and a stereopticon slide show?"

"Oh, Katherine, what would I do without you?" he laughed. "A stereopticon show is merely a succession of slides. We often use them to teach with. We feel that one picture is better than many words and much more effective. You would be surprised at the accolade we have received, even from the very pious denominations."

"Aha," Nana said gleefully, "you mean those verbose deities who constantly embroider their conversation with ecclesiastical commands? Oh ho! I can just see Satan laughing at you slow-witted preachers. For years he has had the jump on you by usurping every fascinating thing in the entertainment field, while you gnat-strainers and camel swallowers pull your coats up over your heads and hide like ostriches."

Before Andrew could get in a word, she went on scathingly. "I guess I've certainly been misled as to what sin really is. I remember we were taught in that little Salvation Army church that sin was a transgression against God or man. I was not taught that it changes form from one generation to another—regardless of all the fanatics who spend most of their waking moments pointing out so-called 'sins' in other people's lives."

Her emotion was suddenly spent. "Andrew," she said wearily, "do you realize how torn I am between my loved ones and the church?" Suddenly she fell silent. Then her voice quavered as she came to the real reason for her tirade. "This morning Henri came back from the sanitarium in Portland. He looks wonderful, almost ten years younger." Andrew could not suppress an exclamation of surprise. "He's staying with Clyde, and guess what! He's promised to go back to his workshop and finish the invention he's working on. Before he left, he swore he would stay sober and earn the right to be a part of your family. Do you realize that he knows his own grandchildren only by sight? Can you imagine how this hurts me, Andrew—that my husband has to *earn* the right to know his own grandchildren? That he cannot know them or be a part of the family until he is first a part of the church? Oh, Andrew, Andrew, it hurts, it hurts . . .." Her words were lost in sobs.

Andrew's own voice shook as he tried to comfort her.

"It's the children whom I want to know him and love him," Katherine said sadly. "I don't care about what the church thinks. I keep thinking how we've all been crucified over Henri and it reminds me that it was the Pharisees who crucified our Lord." Then she hung up the receiver.

Henri came back to Hollywood with his body renewed and a new purpose. But he soon tired of his constricted life and especially of having to feel that he was always on trial for approval. His old cronies sought him out and he was swallowed up in the gay life of the movie crowd. An old friend, a great Shakespearean actor, persuaded the high command at one of the studios to give Henri a chance at directing. Henri had not lost his innate good taste and his artistic touch. His first effort was a tremendous success.

On the heels of such heroes and heroines as Doug Fairbanks and Mary Pickford came the stars of the canine pictures. For Andrew's sake Clyde and Phillip refrained from having any part in the general bonanza, but did begin to raise and train dogs to be actors. Fawn visited their training kennels. Since she could see nothing particularly sinful, she talked Andrew into letting the children visit Clyde's estate to watch the animal actors go through their paces. Soon the brothers became regular visitors to the manse. But their activities in Hollywood were never mentioned. Since Clyde, Phillip, and Henri had all changed their last names, the pastor's family was spared any possible embarrassment. The children had no idea there were movie personalities in their family tree.

About this time Katherine announced that she was tired of being a frump. For years, she said, she had been emotionally torn between trying to please the church and being a loving mother-in-law. But when the question came up as to whether or not the church was going to tell her how to dress, she put her foot down. She knew her relationship with the Lord was in good order, and that her looking chic couldn't change it.

When her metamorphosis was complete, she came over to the manse to call. Her hair was smartly bobbed and she wore a mink fur which Clyde had given her as a birthday present. The color of flesh showed through her sheer silk hose and the high heels of her tiny shoes clicked merrily as she paraded across the hardwood floors into the den. Fawn and Andrew looked up and gaped.

"Mother!" Fawn choked, "what have you done to yourself? You look like an—an actress!"

"Why, thank you, young lady," Nana retorted. "I consider that a compliment." She spun around, patting her hairdo proudly. "All women will be cutting their hair soon."

"Never," Fawn gasped. "Never, never!"

"Absolutely. Never!" Andrew seconded the remark vehemently.

Nana dropped her eyes for a moment and seemed to be thinking up a good defense. Apparently she decided to let it be for she picked up the tail of a mink and examined it microscopically.

"You would think," she said wryly, "these expensive little creatures would at least have the courtesy to grow a more lush tail—they cost enough." She peered up at Fawn and Andrew, her face slightly pink. "Oh pshaw! I refuse to let you intimidate me. You might as well face it, children. The Edwardian period is over. Women are about to be emancipated."

She glanced defiantly at her son-in-law. "Now I suppose the church will brand all us females as devil-possessed." She tapped her foot impatiently. "I'm as orthodox a coward about hell as anyone, but sin and fashion are not the same thing. Someday some of those prissy ladies will stop fainting at the idea of displaying an ankle bone and then, lo and behold, it won't be a sin anymore."

"Katherine, you didn't give me a chance to say anything about your dress and I'm certainly not going to do so after the fact," Andrew said with a chuckle. "In fact, I think that in your nursing, you'll probably find your bob very convenient. But please don't talk my Fawn into cutting her beautiful hair."

"And why not?" interrupted Katherine.

"Every evening she sits on the bed and listens to all of my woes as she brushes and braids it." He looked at Fawn beseechingly. "If she cuts her hair, she won't have to brush it every night and I won't have a captive audience anymore. I might have to talk to myself, and that would be unbearable."

Fawn's face flushed. "Oh, Andrew, go on with you." She got up to make coffee. "Besides," she smiled, "if I cut my hair, I would have to give up all my large, beautiful hats and then what would the ladies in the congregation have to talk about?"

Fawn and Andrew suspected Sistie of using talcum powder on the sly. But they took it calmly, as only one of many signs that the children were growing up. They were also becoming conscious of the new tempo of music sweeping the nation. The newspapers called it jazz. Andrew's name for it was "The Devil Incognito."

Every time Sistie was sure Mamma and Papa were out of the house, she stopped practicing her études and turned instead to beating out this new kind of rhythm. Her fingers flew over the keyboard in wild syncopation as she tried to reproduce the music she had heard at the Long Beach amusement park. Sistie was a natural mimic. With a little practice, she was able to imitate Tin Pan Alley to perfection.

Nana encouraged her. While Sistie played the popular tunes, Katherine would entertain Matthew by doing the highland fling. But she always took great care to explain to her grandchildren the difference between the old country

folk dances and the vulgar goings-on in the public dance
halls. Her warnings weren't necessary. The children were
firmly convinced that drink and dancing were Sodom and
Gomorrah and the Devil had his headquarters somewhere
between the two.

This conviction was unexpectedly strengthened one day.
Andrew had gone into a saloon to talk to the derelicts and
left the children waiting in the Chariot. They knew Papa
would try to maneuver these lost souls to the corner cafe,
sober them up on coffee, then walk them down to the Mission for spiritual counseling.

Suddenly, Papa came bursting through the wide swinging doors. His eyes were wild, his sleeve half torn from his
coat. Screeching and clutching at his coattails was a painted,
bespangled, orange-haired woman. As they watched, she
lunged forward and grabbed Papa by the collar.

"Oh, no you don't, Lover-boy," she squealed posses-
sively. "You come right back here. You're going to buy your
sweetie pie a drink."

"Crank the car, Son," he yelled at Bud. "Crank the
car!"

Bud leaped over the car door, then stopped in his tracks.
He was paralyzed by the sight of the garish woman who
seemed on the point of strangling Papa. Andrew finally
jerked himself free, seized the crank, shoved it into position,
and spun the handle furiously. The motor coughed and
groaned, but it refused to start.

"Get behind the wheel!" Papa shouted. Bud was still
unable to move.

In desperation, Andrew dashed around front of the car,
his female pursuer now hot on his heels. He turned the key
and jerked the spark lever down. Then he ran back and
spun the crank. The woman came after him once more, now
laughing hilariously at his antics. When he came within
reach, she wound one plump bare arm around his waist and

the other about his neck. Then she started pulling him back toward the saloon.

"Come on, Good-looking. Don't play hard to get. Let's get familiar—I like you." The minister was struggling to free himself. The woman's attentions threw him slightly off balance. At that moment the starter caught hold. It spun the crank backwards, catching Andrew across his wrist with a loud, sickening crack. A small gasping cry of agony escaped him. Then he slipped quietly to the ground.

The sight of his beloved Papa limp on the ground released Bud. Furious, he flew at the woman bending over Andrew.

"Go away, you awful thing. Get away from my Papa!" he screamed.

The children climbed out of the car and clustered around. Tears ran down their cheeks.

Lolly was jumping up and down. She howled at the top of her lungs. "She killed him! Papa's dead! Papa's dead! She killed him!" Slowly with much effort, Papa opened his eyes and sat up.

"There, there now darlings. Papa's not dead," he said between clenched teeth. He grabbed his wrist and struggled to keep from fainting.

The children, catching sight of the grotesque bulge of the broken bone, cried even harder. Andrew tried to hide it under his coat.

"Don't worry, children," he said. "A broken bone is nothing—nothing at all." Then he turned to Bud. "Son, you'll have to take charge. Run to the hardware store across the street and call the Hackenburgs. They live close by. Hurry, Son, hurry." Bud spun around on his heel and was off across the street.

The injured man sat leaning against the car. His eyes were shut and his face was white.

The ambulance and the Hackenburgs arrived at almost

the same moment. As the Maxwell drove into sight, they could see old Sarah Hackenburg, who always did the driving, hunched over the wheel. She pulled the automobile over to the curb with screeching brakes, and thrusting her long skirt to one side, she jumped out of the car. Jedadiah Hackenburg followed meekly behind.

Sarah, clucking, leaned over Papa. "Are you badly hurt?" He shook his head. Then she caught sight of the girl from the saloon who had stopped laughing now and was standing there wondering what to do. Sarah smacked the top of her own straw hat, pushing it down over her ears, then turned on the girl with the full fury of her righteous wrath.

"You git away from my pastor!" she screeched. "You git up and git . . . you . . . you daughter of Sodom!"

The girl backed away mumbling apologetically, "How did I know he was a man of the cloth?" She held out her hands imploringly. "He . . . didn't have his collar on backwards." Then she ran back into the saloon.

That evening at the dinner table, Andrew glanced at his arm, resting in a sling, then over at Bud.

"What happened to you today, Son?" he inquired. "Why didn't you move faster? If you had gotten the car cranked in time, I could have escaped that . . . that. . . ."

"Daughter of Sodom," Lolly contributed.

Bud blushed and looked up at his father apologetically. "Inside me I *was* running, Papa, but my legs didn't seem to know it."

18

The Sawdust Trail and the Minister's Kids

Nana always insisted that preachers and chicken dinners were inseparable. Minnie agreed. Around the manse, chickens were either being fed, killed, or cooked, especially when visiting preachers came to town.

Not only the most famous of them all, but also the heartiest eater was the renowned evangelist, Billy Sunday. Billy hit Los Angeles like a cyclone. The newspapers heralded his coming with headlines, followed up by a plethora of anecdotes concerning his career as a former baseball player. Andrew gathered his children around him and read them stories of the man who was to make such an impact on their lives.

Hundreds of people were on hand at the depot when Billy Sunday's train came in. But Jed and Sarah Hackenburg, his longtime friends, had worked their way through the crowd. They were the first to greet him. Jedadiah threw his arms around Billy. As usual, Sarah pounded the top of her hat with enthusiasm and grabbed the famous evangelist around the neck to give him a peck on the cheek. Then Sarah propelled their pastor's children forward.

Sarah introduced them proudly, explaining, "Their Papa is still out at the campgrounds helping the men set up the tent. We're not Presbyterians now," she cackled. "But wait till you meet our preacher and his wife. You'll never know the difference."

The night Billy Sunday opened his meetings, Andrew piled everyone into the Chariot. Before the service began, the children were all lined up on the front benches, making sure they didn't miss anything.

From all over Southern California, thousands of people arrived. Long before Billy himself appeared, the tent was filled to capacity and an extension was hastily erected to seat the overflow.

Homer Rodeheaver was Billy's star singer and trombone player. When he sang, he could be heard a block away. The children thought they would never forget the sound of his glorious voice. But the minute Billy Sunday stepped into the pulpit, they *knew* they would never forget his preaching. From the evangelist's lips sentences almost literally exploded.

He was never still for two seconds. He ran back and forth across the platform, jumped on chairs, then returned and pounded the pulpit. The pastor's children took careful note of this remarkable behavior. They leaned forward on their benches watching every move. They were already preparing to incorporate the evangelist's gyrations into their own basement services. Open-mouthed, they watched in rapt concentration as Billy chased the Devil around the platform, kicking him in the pants while he gave the audience a dollop of Old Time Religion. He quoted Scripture verses at breakneck speed, never once referring to his Bible. At the close of the service, he beat on the pulpit harder than ever and violently urged the audience to forsake sin. They must head down the "sawdust trail" and be converted.

The pastor's children were overcome with emotion. Weeping copiously, they staggered to the altar and fell on their knees. Between prayers, Sistie, Bud, and Lolly kept poking one another and in hoarse whispers, retailing each other's sins. Generously they forgave and rose at last with wet, shining faces. They walked in silence to the Chariot to wait for Mamma and Papa.

On the way home, each could hardly wait for the other's confession to end, before disclosing his own wickedness. Fawn listened to her five offspring, continuously shocked. "Why you children were all converted years ago," she said, after a bit. "You should have left room for real sinners."

Bud stared at her in surprise. "Mamma, how can you say that? We *were* a bunch of dirty sinners, all of us," he said flatly.

One day while Bud was mowing the lawn, he happened to glance in the window of the house next door. There he saw a botle of wine sitting on the table. The sight filled him with concern for the neighbor's souls. He hurried to his room and began to rehearse his next Saturday's sermon in front of a mirror. Recalling everything Billy Sunday had said about Demon Rum, he made notes so that he wouldn't forget.

The next Saturday, Bud ordered the younger children to round up all the spare boxes and chairs they could find. Then he sent them out into the "highways and hedges" to bring all of their friends to the revival.

The transformation of basement into tabernacle was impressive. An old library table donated by a neighbor served as a pulpit. Minnie had been cajoled into providing a pitcher of water and a glass. Just before the service was about to start, Bud ordered the basement windows to be opened wide. He wanted to be sure that his wine-bibbing neighbors profited from his "Hellfire and Damnation" sermon. Sistie played the Offertory on Fawn's little pump organ. Tommy Carton passed around an old chipped plate to receive the offering. Pidge went up and down the aisle handing out some old hymnals he had found stored away in a box in the garage.

Bud took his place in the homemade pulpit. He cleared his throat several times for silence and announced his text.

"He who drinks is damned!" he shouted. While he preached, he pounded the pulpit and yelled toward the open window. "Repent of drink, or perish in the everlasting hell-fire prepared for the devils and his angels."

"Hallelujah!" Duck shouted.

It came time for the altar call. Bud pleaded with his audience to repent and be converted before it was too late.

The neighborhood children were so excited that they all moved up to the altar en masse. Bud pounded one boy on the back and exhorted, "Hold on, brother!"

Duck pounded the same back and entreated, "Let go, brother."

"Hallelujah!" Pidge shouted.

After the service Bud brought the offering upstairs to be dropped in his mite box. Later, Fawn peeked into the bowl and ran her fingers through the objects. She looked at Minnie and laughed.

"They don't appear to have collected much money for the missionaries," she said, "but they certainly did gather in some of the most interesting buttons I ever saw."

On his way home from school, Duck, who was then about six, made a habit of taking a shortcut through a small, old cemetery. Broken headstones with lopsided angels guarded the tombs of the Spaniards and the graves of the early pioneers. Without giving his surroundings second thought, Duck sometimes paused to puzzle out the epitaphs or to pick wild poppies.

One day as he was traipsing through the grounds with an armful of wild flowers for his mother, he saw, leaning against a headstone, a piece of muslin stuffed with something mysterious. Diffidently, Duck picked it up. Then he tucked the remains together reverently, folded the corners of the cloth around the contents and ran joyously home to show Mamma. As he entered the yard, he bumped into Pidge, zooming around a corner of the house in his wagon. Duck held his precious bundle high over his head.

"Pidge, Pidge!" he yelled. "Guess what I found!" He set the bundle down on the ground. He kept his silence long enough to allow Pidge's curiosity to come to a boiling point. Then, in hushed tones, he disclosed his secret.

Pidge leaned down with a skeptical look on his face, and drew back a corner of the cloth with his fingertips.

"Doesn't look like a soul to me," he said.

"It is too a soul," Duck retorted. "Why, I was there watching when it rose right out of a grave. I caught it on its way to heaven." Doubt struggled with credulity on Pidge's face. "Honest Injun, Pidge, those feathers are its wings."

"Really?" His skepticism was beginning to melt before the sheer fascination of Duck's concept. "Do you think it might fly away if you give it a chance?"

Duck pondered the idea for a moment. "No-o," he said. "We have to wait until it's dark. Nobody ever saw a soul go up to heaven. So it must be dark when they go."

"Don't you think we ought to have a funeral and sing something before it goes?" Pidge inquired thoughtfully.

"Sure," Duck nodded his head with enthusiasm. "Let's get all the kids and have a real funeral. We haven't had anything to bury for a long time."

Whenever word went around the neighborhood that there was to be a funeral at the preacher's house, the yard

was filled instantly. When it came to a funeral service,
nobody could hold a candle to the preacher's kids. They
held funerals for goldfish, for birds, for frogs, and even
large bugs. And their services were conducted with a flair,
with an eye for detail, which any prominent undertaker
would have regarded with envy. For the coffin, the children used everything from a matchbox or cereal container
to a packing box or whatever would fit both the cadaver and
the occasion. They lined the boxes with cotton and covered
them with material stealthily filched from their mother's
sewing drawer.

Pidge rounded up the youngsters, while Duck tiptoed
upstairs to get the materials for making the casket. When
Duck came down with his precious bundle, they all lined
up to view the remains. Tommy Carton had the temerity
to take a peek inside the cloth.

"That ain't no soul," he said in a loud brassy voice.
"Souls are supposed to be pretty. This one stinks!"

Duck and Pidge both shouted at him. "That soul does
not stink. It's sacrilegious to say so."

"Here, look at the wings," Duck insisted, carefully
unfolding the cloth. "It was all ready to fly to heaven.
Doesn't that prove it's a soul?"

Tommy gingerly lifted back the muslin again and
started to poke about.

"Don't touch it!" Duck cried out in a voice filled with
alarm.

Arnold Murphy, another neighbor boy, looked into the
cracker box coffin, and squinted at Tommy. "A preacher's
kid ought to know a soul when he sees one, if anybody
does," he mused. "Don't you know that, you idiot?"

"I guess so," Tommy said contritely, subdued by the
overwhelming weight of the evidence against him.

Pidge shoved the kids into a line. Suddenly he snapped
his fingers.

"Duck," he said, in a shocked voice, "we almost forgot the flowers." Hastily he yanked up some of Fawn's geraniums by the roots and passed them down the line of mourners.

Duck stood at the head of the line and the children formed a queue behind him. They started to move forward, but he held up his hand and stopped them.

"Since this is a soul funeral, I'd better get Papa's swallow-tailed suit. Wait for me."

Duck dashed up to his father's closet, pulled the Sunday coat from the hanger, and carefully folded it over his arm. Just then his eyes caught sight of a motto hanging over Papa's dresser which read, "The Just Shall Live by Faith." Knowing that Mamma was nowhere around, Duck lifted the motto from the hook and ran down the stairway with it.

"I got a headstone!" he called out. "Now we can make a real grave." He hurried to the head of the line.

Pidge handed him a hymnbook. "What do you want us to sing?" he asked. "Something special?" Opening the book at random, Pidge stepped out of line and answered his own question.

" 'Jesus Loves Me!' That's the only one everybody knows," he said. "Now when you sing, try to look sad," he went on. "And be sure you pull on your Adam's apple. That will make your voice wiggle and make it sound just like Caruso. I heard him once, so I know."

"It doesn't make your voice wiggle," Duck corrected him. "It makes it tremble."

Duck held the precious casket in his arms and looked down the line.

"Now when I start walking, you guys sing . . . and sing good and mournfully." He started around the side of the house.

At that moment, Fawn and Andrew drove up in the Chariot. They sat quietly in the car, watching the sad-faced procession. Each mourner was plucking at the skin on his throat. As they rounded the house for the third time, their voices came out wiggling in wild discord.

The pastor smiled broadly and beamed at the whole idea. Then he noticed that Duck was wearing his coat and dragging the tails through the grass. He also observed that every few steps, as Pidge caught up with Duck, he would step firmly on one of the tails.

Duck saw his parents, stopped the procession, and approached the car. His brown eyes lit up. "Papa!" he exclaimed, "we're having a funeral for a soul. You weren't here to ask, but I just knew you'd want me to wear your best coat."

Andrew frowned and opened his mouth to speak. His wife tugged at his sleeve and shook her head. Papa closed his mouth and stared wordlessly, glancing at the bundle Duck held lovingly in his arms. He couldn't help noticing that blood was oozing over the sleeve. One of the pieces of burlap fell aside and Andrew got a good look at the cadaver.

"What in the world . . ." he exclaimed, and then took off on another tack. "Look what you're doing to my best coat. It will be ruined. Take it off immediately."

Duck tenderly recovered the box and then held up a hand. "Please don't talk so loud," he admonished his father. "You are in the presence of a real soul—and one that is in process of departing." Then he softened slightly. "Of course, if you would like to preach a little, it would be all right with us."

Hastily, the pastor shook his head. Fawn motioned him into the house. She was sure if Andrew hung around, he would preach a sermon all right, but the subject would be a coat—rather than a soul.

Outside, the children were singing at the top of their lungs, their voices rising, then falling. Finally they headed

out toward the orchard. Duck stopped the procession long
enough to run to the stables and get a shovel.

"Each one of us gets to dig one shovelful," he said,
laying his burden gently on the ground.

"We better be careful not to dig too deep—or we could
hit China," Tommy warned.

"Hell's down there, too," Pidge reminded them. "Right
under China. We don't want to put the soul in hell. It
might have a hard time getting out."

Duck wagged an admonishing finger at his younger
brother. "Don't say that bad word," he said, "especially at a
funeral."

The last spadeful of earth was patted down over the
casket. Tommy was allowed to put the headstone in place
while the other children all stood around in an awestruck
circle, their faces expressing varying degrees of solemnity.
Johnny Holmes summed up the feelings of the congregation.

"Best funeral I ever went to," he stated firmly. "Let's
have another one tomorrow."

In the den, Fawn was sewing and Andrew was fidgeting about in his morris chair.

"Reverend," said Fawn, "I know what's on your mind.
Stop worrying about the coat. I'll send it to the cleaners if
it needs it."

Andrew looked helplessly at his wife. "It isn't the coat
that I'm worried about, darling," he lamented. "I'm just
trying to figure out how I'm going to break the news to
Duck that he's held a state funeral for the entrails of a
white leghorn chicken."

Social diplomacy was something on which the pastor's
children had cut their teeth. They were taught from baby-
hood how to behave under any circumstances. Sometimes,

however, the lesson was something they could learn only
through bitter experience.

One day after school Duck ran all the way home to ask if
he could spend the afternoon and evening with a friend. He
dashed across the front yard, never for one moment thinking
of Mamma's strictly enforced rule: Never enter the house
by the front door unless accompanied by an adult.

He lunged through the door, burst into the front room,
and stood panting for breath.

Fawn and Andrew were sitting in the front room, entertaining a large man with a bald head who was laughing
uproariously while delicately balancing a cup of coffee on
his knee.

Duck's parents stared at him with surprise and concern.
Duck was usually so careful to come in the back door. The
rotund gentleman looked at the bewildered boy and laughed
even harder than before.

"How do you do, young man?" he bellowed, extending
a big hand.

Duck shyly put forth his own which was promptly en-
gulfed. The small boy's eyes got all teary as he looked toward
his parents.

"I'm sorry," he whispered. "I was in such a hurry, I—I
forgot and came in the wrong door. I didn't know we had
company."

Andrew stood up and put his hand on his son's shoulder.
"Mr. Bryan, I want you to meet one of my million-dollar
boys. This is Wendell. We call him Duck."

The friendly stranger rose and patted the top of Duck's
head. "Fine boy, fine boy," he roared. "Looks every inch a
preacher's son."

Duck mumbled his thanks and excused himself quickly.
With rapid steps, he marched up the stairs with a very
straight back. Fawn was right behind him, as he had sus-

pected she would be. She followed him to his room and
shut the door behind them.

"Duck, you know we have rules for particular reasons."

Duck's head bobbed slowly.

"Just now," Fawn continued, "you could have embarrassed your Papa and me very seriously. There is a certain
protocol, shall we say, that a minister's family must learn.
The absolute privacy of the living room, the den, and
Papa's office is part of that protocol. Papa and I must be
able to entertain guests and counsel people without worrying whether you children will interrupt or overhear our
conversations. Fortunately, Mr. Bryan is a very warm and
generous man. He didn't mind."

Fawn took out her handkerchief and wiped away the
tears that had crawled down Duck's face. "Now, what was
so important that you, of all the children, should break
our rule?"

Duck sniffed and swallowed hard. "I just wanted to know
if I could go over to Jack's house," he said apologetically,
"and play ball this afternoon. His mamma asked me to stay
for supper tonight, too."

"Darling, if you had only come in the back door and
sent Minnie to motion for me, I would have gladly given
permission. But you must learn not to interrupt when adults
are talking."

"Then I never would get to talk around here."

"Hush, I'm not finished." Fawn held up her hand.
"You're to stay here in your room and think about the rule
you have broken. I hate to punish you, Ducky; you seldom
need it. But this time it is necessary. Don't be too disappointed. The gentleman downstairs is a very distinguished person. His name is William Jennings Bryan. He's
called the Silver-Tongued Orator! He's come to speak at
the University. We're going to have him stay for dinner.

I'll call Jack's mother and tell her you won't be able to come."

Duck threw himself onto the bed and gave way to an excess of self-pity. "I'd rather have gone to Jack's. Goodness gracious!" he quoted Papa with gusto. "Mercy sakes alive. Hallelujah!"

The honored guest not only ate well, but between courses he related amusing stories for the children's benefit. At the end of each anecdote he would so shake with laughter that the gold chain danced up and down on his vest. After telling one particularly funny story, Mr. Bryan leaned far back and let out a great guffaw. Quickly, Pidge stood up on his chair and peered down into Mr. Bryan's mouth.

"Pidge, sit down this minute," Andrew remonstrated.

Pidge dropped back down, then turned to Duck. "You told me he had a silver tongue," Pidge said accusingly. "He doesn't either. It's just as red as mine."

At this, Mr. Bryan laughed so hard he almost went over backwards. Luckily for Pidge, his mamma and papa were laughing too hard to be angry.

19

"The Distresses of Choice"

Mechanically Andrew placed the telephone receiver back on the hook. His expression was one of conflicting emotions. In a moment he got up. He found Fawn making the beds. Grinning, trying to be nonchalant, he went over to her and kissed her.

"What would you say if that kiss was a magic one, making you the first lady of Pasadena College?" he inquired. Fawn's head jerked up; the pillow fell to the floor. Her eyes searched Andrew's face.

"Andrew," she murmured, "what in the world . . ."

Andrew swallowed hard. "You knew Doctor Walker was very ill," he said. "Well, he died yesterday."

"Oh, that's a shame," said Fawn.

"The president of the board just called me. I have been elected President of Pasadena College by unanimous vote."

She put her arms around him. "What a very great honor! Isn't it too bad it has to be accompanied by such sorrow?"

"The school has lost a great Bible scholar, a great man," Andrew said. "The Presbyterians certainly gave us an outstanding human being in Doctor Walker." Fawn stiffened, squeezing her husband with her elbows.

"But our church—Andrew—our church. What are you going to do?" Andrew looked out the window for a moment. He took her arms from his waist. His eyes were full of anguish. He began to pace the floor.

"I think we should wait to decide," he said. "I have always felt when the war was over, we might go to—to India. I have waited so long."

"I know," she whispered.

"We shall pray for guidance," he went on. "We certainly cannot let the devil gerrymander a premature decision."

"Why don't we ask God for a token? Perhaps put out the fleece as Gideon did when he went to battle against the Midianites."

"Yes, let us pray that God gives us peace of mind about India if we are to go, that will be our fleece."

"If the same thing works about the school, you will take the Presidency?"

"Yes, I will consider the fleece is wet."

Andrew returned to his den and called the president of the board of trustees of the school to tell him of his decision.

"We will wait to hear from you for one week," the man said. "In the meantime, we shall pray. The school needs you, Doctor." He put the case before them.

Andrew's compassion spilled over and touched everyone with whom he came in contact. Since study for his master's degree at the University of Southern California, he had been involved in a vigorous campaign toward understanding between the educators and the church. "Would this election to the Presidency of Pasadena College give him an opportunity to continue his campaign on another front?"

During the week Andrew met at the church with his elders, board of deacons, and trustees.

"We feel strongly that your work is not finished here, Pastor," Doctor Kirkland said. "I sincerely think we will be

in jeopardy if you leave. Although you have your D.D.,
you're working for your Ph.D. Don't you think it would be
wise to wait?"

Andrew felt checkmated in every direction. Wearily he
cranked the Chariot and started home. Rounding the corner
of Wall Street, he saw Doctor Paul Bresee driving toward
him. The doctor leaned over the side of his touring car and
called, "I want to talk to you, Andrew. I'll follow you
home."

The minister turned into the driveway; Doctor Paul
pulled up to the curb in front of the manse. Andrew and
Dr. Bresee entered the front door together. They could hear
Fawn singing in the front room.

"I'd like Fawn to hear this too," the doctor said. At the
sound of their voices, Fawn spun around on the piano stool.

"All right, out with it," she said, "before I die of curiosity."

Andrew motioned them into his study and closed the
door. When they were comfortably seated, Doctor Paul
began.

"Andrew," he said accusingly, "have you forgotten the
deathbed promise you made Father?"

The pastor's dark eyes flamed. "Paul," he expostulated.

The doctor put up his hand to stop him. "Let me finish,"
he said. "You promised Father you would not only give
your life for the church, but for the school. Many of Father's friends in the Methodist and Episcopal churches have
come into our denomination. We have far more ministers
than we ever dared to dream of. But," he went on spiritedly,
"we have very few educators. A man can be found to fill
your pulpit but not to fill the Presidency of the school.
Someday people will realize, as you have, an education is
important—imperative. At the moment the reservoir is
dry."

He looked soberly at Andrew's drawn face. "What do

you consider the most important?" he demanded. "An afflu-
ent church? A dream of being a missionary? Or a deathbed
promise that will serve all the church instead of just a
portion?"

He took his gold watch from his vest pocket and looked
at it. "I have calls to make," he said. He rose from the
couch. "I will expect to hear from you tonight."

Dr. Paul left. Fawn and Andrew knelt beside the davenport. While Andrew prayed, he seemed to once again see
Doctor Phineas Bresee sitting at his big oak desk the night
he had preached the sermon on St. Stephen. Andrew seemed
again to hear the throaty, eloquent voice saying, "Andrew,
God never makes a mistake. But people who hurry on ahead
of him often do." Andrew rose from his knees and wiped
his eyes. He leaned over, put his hands under Fawn's arms,
pulled her to her feet, and kissed her.

"I christen thee the President's Lady," he said.

Fawn looked up into his face. "I see the fleece got wet—
with tears," she said.

She put her arms around him and looked up at him.
"Andrew," she reasoned, "we can still go to the mission
field—when the children are grown and the school is on its
feet." She gave him a squeeze. "Have you forgotten our
wedding song, Drew? 'Whither Thou Goest.' "

Andrew held Fawn close to his heart. "Oh, darling,
how I *agapé* and *philia* thee," he whispered.

20

Mamma's Pink Extravagance

The war had wrought great changes in the culture of Los Angeles. The tail end of the Edwardian period was slipping into history, and Californians were flirting with a radical change in their way of life. Informality was taking over.

The day of the sparkling white linen tablecloth with the centerpiece of fresh flowers, the crystal, silver, and hand-painted china were all relegated to the sideboards to catch dust. Servants were vanishing, too. But the appearance of such labor-saving devices as washing machines and dish-washers cushioned the shock.

Fawn didn't want any new gadgets, but there was one thing she did want . . . and she wanted it desperately—a newfangled davenport to seat more people. What's more, although it must be a real bargain, she wanted an elegant one for a change. It had to be pink . . . preferably pink brocade with fringe on the bottom and tassels hanging from the arms exactly like one she had seen on a billboard. The sheer audacity of her desire sent a shudder through her. Then she managed to rationalize her yearnings by mentally seating on her pink davenport a deaconess or missionary, primly sipping tea. Her mental picture looked so proper that she quickly conquered her guilt feelings. She began to save her teaching money, squirreling it away where her husband couldn't find it.

Matters came to a head one afternoon when she stood in the doorway of Andrew's den watching him tie up the springs of the big old black leather couch. He looked up at her and grinned.

"One of these days you're going to have to get that new couch you've wanted for such a long time," Andrew said. "This thing is about to give up the ghost."

"I do happen to have a little teaching money put away . . . if you haven't gotten into it," Fawn said casually. "Maybe we could find a davenport at one of those auctions that Buffington's holds. Several women have told me they bought exquisite furniture there for nothing . . . Well, almost nothing," she amended hastily.

"Don't you think we should have one that turns into a bed?" Papa offered. "You know how we're always needing an extra place to put people."

Fawn found the very thought appalling. She could see the pink sofa quickly subsiding into a broken-down heap like the leather one.

"One of these days," Fawn said stiffly, "just once, I am going to own something that I don't have to share with other people. And when I do . . . it's going to be pink." She walked down the hall and then shouted back at her husband, "Yes, pink—and satin, too!" Andrew looked up in puzzlement. He had no idea what was bothering her.

For weeks, Fawn watched the newspaper for the advertisement of auction sales at Buffington's. She ran her finger down the list of items, until in the middle of the page, she came to "Pink brocade sofa, sleeps two."

She literally ran up the stairs to her room, reached far to the back of a dresser drawer and took out a small square raffia box. Her hands shook as she counted out the bills. "Fifty-seven dollars," she whispered. "Is that all!" She fell on her knees by the bed. "Lord, I implore you, please help me get that sofa . . . you know I won't be selfish about letting people sleep on it."

The day of the auction, Fawn nervously got herself all dressed up. Standing in front of the mirror, she glanced down at her plain navy blue dress. "Mercy, I certainly do need new clothes," she said. Then shaking off her moment of doubt, "Oh, but I'd *much* rather have the sofa!"

That afternoon the three older children were walking up the driveway on their way home from school, when Sistie suddenly noticed something through the front window, something new—and pink.

"Look," she yelled, "Mamma did get it. She really did. Doesn't it look beautiful in the window?"

"Snazzy," Lolly said excitedly.

During the week, the family noticed that whenever Mamma had a moment to spare, she would slip into the front room to admire her new possession. She would run her hands lovingly over the silken fabric, then fluff the down pillows. At night just before retiring, she would stand in front of the pink apparition and just gaze at it in rapture.

"Do you think we'll ever get to sit on our new sofa?" Duck asked Minnie one night as she was washing his face.

"Oh! Yah, someday," she assured him, "when de new iss off."

One beautiful sunny morning Fawn left to preside at a missionary meeting. She took the Chariot, leaving Andrew in the den tutoring a student. A few minutes later, his lesson was interrupted by the ringing of the telephone. He frowned as he realized that it was Mrs. Portsmouth, one of the most incorrigible beggars of his flock.

"Reverend," came her pleading whine, "I'm turning to

you for help. Poor Nina—that's my oldest married daughter —is having a baby again."

"M-mm," said the preacher warily, not knowing what was coming, but on his guard.

"She simply must have an extra bed. *Surely* you know of someone in the church who might loan us a couch or something—at least until her poor husband gets another job."

Andrew tried to soothe Mrs. Portsmouth, telling her not to worry. He was sure he could find a bed for Nina. The minute she hung up, knowing he would no longer be able to concentrate, he brought the lesson to an end. Then he began phoning members of the church to inquire about a bed. The story was the same: there were no beds. Everyone knew Nina—everyone that is, but her minister. Any bed loaned to that family probably would never be returned. Even if such an unlikely thing *did* happen, the bed would be in such a deplorable condition as to be fit only for the junkyard.

Eventually Andrew called Mrs. Portsmouth back and broke the unhappy news. He had been totally unable to locate a bed.

"But—but," begged Mrs. Portsmouth—she paused as she prepared to play her trump card. "I understand that you have a brand new davenport—and it's one that turns into a bed. Surely you wouldn't deny a needy family a place to sleep when you have so many lovely beds. Would you want poor Nina's babies to make-do on the floor?"

Andrew hesitated for a moment—a long, long moment. He thought of Fawn and how she had scrimped and saved to buy that pink delight. He thought of the way she stopped every night before going to bed to look at it lovingly. But Mrs. Portsmouth—Nina—the unborn baby—his shoulders drooped.

"Very well," he said at last in a voice filled with resignation, "you may borrow our sofa for a few days. But please take very good care of it. My wife has wanted this piece of furniture for years. She earned the money to buy it herself." His voice trailed off. The receiver was dead.

Later that afternoon Mrs. Portsmouth and her husband drove up in front of the manse. Their dilapidated old car was followed closely by an equally dilapidated old trailer.

Andrew helped the couple load the pink sofa. In the dirty trailer, it looked strangely, splendidly sad, like royalty fallen from grace, and on the way to the guillotine in a hand-me-down tumbril.

As they started to leave, Mrs. Portsmouth turned to her minister. "Oh, Doctor, do you happen to have a little extra bedding? I'm sure Nina will return it as soon as Joe gets on his feet."

Andrew went back into the house, peered in the linen closet, and took out four sheets. He hurried out to the car and handed them to Mrs. Portsmouth. She thanked him sweetly. Then suddenly, as though a new thought had just struck her, she added, "Oh, gracious me, I forgot to mention quilts! Do you have any old, worn-out quilts you won't miss for a few days?"

Back upstairs went Andrew, on the prowl for extra quilts. Not finding any, he started to go outside to the storeroom in the stables. As he walked down the hall, he noticed, folded up at the foot of the girl's beds, two down-filled taffeta comforters. Furthermore they were pink, a perfect match for the davenport. Delighted, he grabbed them and ran downstairs.

"My goodness sakes alive!" Mrs. Portsmouth exclaimed, as he handed them to her, "aren't these beautiful? It's a surprise to me that a minister can afford such luxury!"

Andrew's face went stony. "My good mother-in-law

made those quilts from a featherbed," he said coldly. "Fawn
takes special care of them, as she does all of our things.
And I expect you to do the same."

A little while later, Fawn drove the Chariot up the
driveway. Getting out, she noticed something peculiar.
Through the window she could see the big old library table.
That seemed strange. Usually the pink sofa was in the way.
She passed a hand over her eyes and muttered to herself.

"Now that's funny. I would have warranted I saw a
couch from the window as I drove out. I wonder why Minnie moved it." She ran into the house and hurried to the
front room. The sofa was not there. In its place stood the
library table. She ran wildly from room to room. There was
no pink sofa to be seen anywhere.

For a moment, she stood at the foot of the stairs, her
hands over her face.

"Oh, what could have happened to it?" Finally she
found her voice. "Andrew," she called, "Andrew, where
are you?"

Her husband poked his head around the door of his den,
"Lover, is that you?"

"The sofa!" Fawn squeaked. "Someone has stolen my
sofa."

Andrew took a long time to close his door and walk
down the hall. He could feel his wife's anxious eyes upon
him. He avoided her gaze. He cleared his throat several
times.

"Darling, ahem," he said, stalling for time. "Ahem . . .
Nina Portsmouth, ahem, is having another . . . baby."

"Yes," Fawn sighed. Her voice seemed far away. "But
what's that got to do with my pink sofa?"

"They needed a bed desperately." He extended his
hands imploringly, "I didn't want to do it . . . I called several people . . . no one had a bed." He shook his head

miserably. "I was forced to loan them our . . . your sofa."

"Loan!" Fawn uttered a cry of pure anguish. "Surely you know about the Portsmouths. They never give anything back—and if they do it'll be a wreck. They'll let the children ruin it. They ruin every stick of furniture they possess." She burst forth with sobs. "My beautiful pink sofa! It won't be worth two cents when they get through with it."

As she spoke tears dropped down and spotted her navy blue suit.

Andrew went to her and tried to put his arm around her.

"Fawn, I'm so sorry," he said contritely, "I guess this time I was too hasty." Fawn pulled quickly away. Andrew went on with his confession. "The Portsmouths would have found a bed somewhere, I'm afraid they have leaned on us and the church for so long, the next thing you know, they'll expect the church to support them." He cocked his head and forced a wan, but appealing boyish smile.

"Forgive me darling . . . please?"

Fawn knew her weakness. She avoided looking at his face and gave him no answer. Slowly she mounted the stairs, walked to her room, threw herself on the bed, and wept.

Andrew, who had followed her up the stairs, remained standing awkwardly in the doorway. There was a weight upon his soul. He had still more to confess.

"Fawn, that woman not only got the sofa," he said miserably. Before he could say more, he saw his wife's form stiffen, as though seized with a convulsion. "She had nothing to put over it. I had to give her some sheets and coverlets."

Fawn half-raised herself from the bed so that she could turn her tear-stained face. "What sheets? What coverlets?" she asked fearfully.

"The sheets were from the guest closet," Papa's voice

trembled slightly. "I took the extra down comforters off Sistie's and Lolly's beds."

Fawn, twisting her head around, stared at him in disbelief. She placed her fingers over her mouth and whispered unbelievingly, "Oh no . . . my new percale sheets. Those lovely taffeta comforters. The ones my mother made for me! Why, Andrew? . . . Why did you do it?"

She stared at the floor and seemed to be talking to herself. "Mother worked for months quilting those comforters. They're so beautiful. I've never even used them. I've been saving them for extra special guests."

Andrew went over to the bed and stood above her. Then he sat down, pulled her over to him, and held her tight. She remained catatonically rigid, totally unresponsive to his caress.

Suddenly his attitude underwent a complete change. He got up and strode toward the door. There he stopped, turned, and frowned at her.

"Fawn," he said sternly, "I'm shocked. This is the first time I have ever seen any selfishness in you." He waited for his tactic to take effect.

Fawn sat up abruptly; tears were flowing down her face as she looked at Andrew in disbelief. "Selfish, you say I'm selfish because it hurts me to give lovely things to . . . to . . . people who have no feeling for them. Aren't they more selfish to ask? Ever since we've been married I have never owned anything beautiful for long; someone always finagled it out of you . . . somehow. Giving away the few things I love to people who won't help themselves." The floodgates of her emotions opened wide now and words poured out.

"All my life I've had to hide my cold cream in the bottom of the wastebasket because people came snooping into our bathroom. They even looked for the price tags on the bottoms of the jars. I've caught them at it." Regally she

held up her hand as Andrew's mouth opened. He closed it
and she continued. "I've never been allowed to wear my
engagement chain out where everyone could see it. Why?
Because it might offend someone. I have had to explain to
every envious woman in the congregation that I didn't go
to the beauty parlor—that my hair is naturally curly. And
I had to try to prove it."

Her voice broke. "I have given up all claim on my husband's time. And if you can say that's being selfish, God
forgive me, I just don't know the meaning of the word." She
caught her breath. "I even think, if it wasn't immoral, there
are times you would have given *me* away." She began crying again.

Andrew turned and walked silently down the hall. He
took a handkerchief from his pocket and dabbed at his eyes.
As he thought it over he could see she was right. What he
had looked upon as being so unselfish and full of *agapé* had
hurt the one person who did not deserve it. He was wrong.
This was not *agapé* at all; it was a foolish compulsion to
keep people happy and perhaps get himself off the hook,
all at Fawn's expense. The blood seemed to drain from him
and he felt cold.

The more he thought, the worse he felt. His feet were
heavy as he trudged down the stairway toward his den. He
stood silently by the door for a moment trying to think
things out. Then he went to his big leather chair, slumped
down in it, and let his breath out slowly. His high stiff
collar seemed to choke him. He jerked off his tie, pulled the
collar off and ran a finger around the neckband of his shirt;
then he reached for the telephone and gave the operator
Katherine's number.

While he waited, he tormented himself with pangs of
remorse. His mind went back to the many sacrifices Fawn
had made for him and for the family—the material sacrifices

and the spiritual ones. Now that he thought of it, she had even changed her nature; she had made herself an extrovert for his sake, to be a better preacher's wife and had never complained. Why, she had even given her wedding band, her most precious possession, to the heathen. He groaned aloud and rolled his eyes to heaven. And he, thoughtless soul, had been so consumed with being unselfish, that he hadn't even taken the trouble to replace it.

"Oh, eternity be thou my refuge. I should be horse-whipped," he moaned.

That evening Fawn did not come down for dinner. There was a heavy silence at the table. Even Matthew with his anecdotes couldn't shoo the clouds from the children's faces. Andrew kept his eyes glued on his plate and averted his gaze when anyone glanced in his direction. While he read the Scripture, his voice was toneless. When he finished, he lowered his head and pressed his fingers tightly against his temples.

Minnie hurried the children from the table and up to their rooms. Andrew sat unmoving at the empty table. He was still there when Nana arrived.

Her first words when she walked in the door were, "Where's your new sofa? Don't you like it in front of the window anymore?"

Her son-in-law winced. "Sit down," he said. "That's what I wanted to talk to you about." He sat playing with his fork. "Katherine, I've done something terrible. Let's go into the den where we can talk. It's unforgivable and I need help."

In the den, he indicated a big rocker to Nana. Then he dropped into his morris chair, averting his face as he spoke. To Katherine, he seemed to become smaller and smaller as he narrated the events of the day. Suddenly he looked up.

"I don't even like those Portsmouths . . . if I think of

them in the flesh," he reasoned. "But when I think of what a nothing I am and my Lord gave his life because he loved me—I am forced to *agapé* them, dirt and all." He looked up sheepishly. "I guess I go overboard on everything. You know me, no halfway stuff. And I have no excuse," he mumbled shaking his head. "I'm the one that's selfish."

A pathetic look spread over his face and he let out a big sigh. "I not only gave Fawn's new pink couch—I went the whole hog. I gave them—lo-loaned them—four new sheets and those . . . those wonderful comforters you made for the girls," he groaned.

Katherine shook her head incredulously and clucked her tongue. Then she sat back for a moment and stared at her son-in-law before she went on. Her dark eyes flashed. "This time, Andrew, you have gone too far. I never dreamed you could stay so gullible all these years." She shook her finger at him. "All through the years, I have seen you two kids scrimp and save and make-do, just so you could give, give, give."

She jumped to her feet and gestured. "Just because you live in this house you seem to have a guilty conscience. You seem to forget you won't be here forever. I'm sure God loves a cheerful giver. And I'm just as sure he hates a chronic taker. I've kept silent while you youngsters have given of yourselves to the bone—your money, your time, your energy. That's your business. But giving that hurts someone besides yourself can be cruel."

She turned sharply. "Remember when Doctor Easton was here? Well, I cringe, Andrew, when I remember how Fawn took off her wedding ring and placed it on the altar. That was her most cherished possession. Did I say anything when you were so entranced with that man's experience that every conversation you had with Fawn began, 'Now in India . . .' You hoped, didn't you, that she would be converted to donning a pith helmet post haste, and dragging five children into the black hole of Calcutta. Thank God she had sense enough to wait for a call from the Lord and not mistake your prodding for his voice. Sometimes people need to stop giving and take for a change."

She stopped and looked hard at Andrew. When she continued her voice was more gentle. "You're both going to have to stop some of this bloodletting or you'll soon need a transfusion yourselves. Not only for the sake of your body, but for the sake of your soul." She paused. "I always gave you credit for understanding women. Now I guess I overestimated your intelligence.

"Doesn't that fancy course in psychology at the University teach you that the food of the soul is far more important to some people than three meals a day? Remember," she said nodding, "a pastor's wife has to face all of the vicissitudes of life without any of the anointment of praise that her husband gets poured on his head every day."

Andrew winced. He had been expecting some sort of lecture, but he wasn't prepared for this biting barrage.

Nana knew when she had philosophized enough. Her first burst of anger past, she returned to her chair and clasped her hands together.

"I've just said what I've been wanting to say for a long time," she declared. She leaned forward to Andrew and spoke softly. "Let me tell you a story about an aged Negress on my father's plantation, when I was a little girl," she began.

"One night I ran away from home. I thought I was lost and I was scared. I saw an open door and I galloped up that porch into the house like the devil was after me and ran smack dab into an old woman sitting in a rocker right in the center of the floor. She didn't say a word. She just reached out and scooped me up in her arms. She held me tight, then she began to hum. Finally I stopped shaking and she began to sing. She sang on and on. Hours later my father found me. When I got down from her lap in the dim light, I saw that old woman was barefoot. I don't know why, but I reached down and touched one of her feet. It was cold as ice. I never forgot those poor cold feet. Often at night when I was snuggled in my bed, I worried about that old woman's feet. I finally told my mother and she gave me a dollar to take down to her so she could have someone buy her a pair of shoes. Later when I went back to see her I expected to see her wearing warm slippers. She was still barefoot. When I asked her what she had done with the money, she looked at me a moment and then pointed to a pink geranium in a bright hand-painted pot. She said something I shall never forget as long as I live. I want you to remember it too, Andrew. That dear old woman said, 'My feet ain't as important as my soul.'"

Nana waited a moment for the remark to sink in. "I, too, found out early in life that food, shelter, and clothes don't always fill a person's needs. Sometimes we need a pink geranium."

Andrew pushed his fingers against his misty eyes. He shook his head. "Oh! Katherine, what have I done to my precious little Fawn? Help me, help me think of some way to make amends. I'm so ashamed. I didn't dream I was giving away something as necessary as a . . . pink geranium."

"Well, one thing I can say for sure," Nana went on, "you were suitably named. You will do anything to bring people to the Lord, even if it hurts your loved ones. Andrew the Apostle brought people to Jesus, by hook or crook. But even in the Bible it doesn't say he gave them everything he had. Now why couldn't you have been a little more like the Apostle Matthew?"

"Katherine, you know not only did Matthew give banquets so the rich could hear Jesus, eventually he sold all that he had and followed his Lord."

"I was afraid you would bring that up." Nana winked at Andrew. "Now you're going to learn that you have more than two actors in the family," she said, "because right now I am going upstairs and stage the best act you ever saw. Put the coffee on and while I am emoting, you might as well start rehearsing the speech you are going to deliver to that Portsmouth woman tomorrow."

"Wha—What speech?" stammered Andrew.

"You are going after that sofa . . . and the sheets . . . and the quilts . . ." She punctuated each phrase with a none-too-gentle shove at Andrew's chest. "And you're not going to come home unless you bring them with you." Then she straightened her shoulders and marched up the stairway.

Katherine found her daughter lying on her back across the bed, staring at the ceiling. She shook a finger at Fawn accusingly.

"Do you mean to tell me that you are up here wallowing around in self-pity while that darling husband of yours is down there eating his heart out? I'm ashamed of you. I didn't raise you to act like a spoiled brat. You know Andrew didn't have a chance against that Portsmouth woman."

"Oh, Mother, you know how I love Andrew and appreciate his deep and abiding *agapé*, but something in me always sees a boundary as to how much each individual should give. My poor pink sofa," she sniffed, with a heart-rending sigh of resignation.

Katherine, although greatly moved, broke in on Fawn's mood, briskly. "You knew how warm and generous Andrew was before you married him. You shouldn't come complaining now that you've discovered he's *consistent*."

"Yes, I know . . . oh, I know, it's just hard sometimes. My sofa. . ."

"I don't want to hear another word about your sofa. I have a feeling you're going to see that sofa again very shortly," Katherine stated firmly. "Now I want you to go into the bathroom, wash your face, and put on some powder so you'll look a little less like a witch. Then go downstairs and apologize for acting like a spoiled baby."

Still reluctant, but more or less resigned, Fawn got up and went into the bathroom.

Nana flopped down on the bed and ran a hand over her eyes. "Whew," she muttered, "I never dreamed that playing both sides against the middle could be so exhausting." She quietly left the room, tiptoed down the stairway, and out the front door.

Fawn powdered her face. Then she stood in front of the mirror, puffed her hair, pinched her cheeks, and tried to think of an apology.

Andrew lingered at the bottom of the stairs. He wanted to go up to her, but he couldn't seem to find the right words.

Fawn walked slowly down the hall to the top of the stairs. She saw her husband and stopped, suddenly shy.

Andrew looked up at her. "Fawn . . . I."

She ran down the stairway.

Andrew charged up the stairs two at a time.

There was nothing they really needed to say.